The Scarecrows Will Watch Over Us

Grant Wamack

Broken River Books

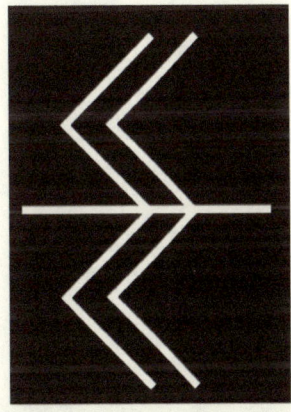

A Broken River Books Original
BROKEN RIVER BOOKS
Oklahoma City, OK
Copyright ©2025 Grant Wamack

Cover art by Don Noble
https://roosterrepublicpress.com/covers/
Edited by Xavier Garcia
xavier.garcia.gallardo@gmail.com
Interior layout design by Kelby Losack
https://kelbylosack.com/

ISBN: 978-1-940885-73-5

Printed in the U.S.A.

"Though it has no thought of keeping watch, it's not for naught that the scarecrow stands in the grain field."

—Dogen

SOME PEOPLE CALLED GARY a vagabond, a title he enjoyed and carried with great pride, while others called him a traveling man. Some called him homeless, or unhoused—a new word that made him feel less than empowered. But most people called him a bum. A term that made his neck muscles tense as he spat on the cracked asphalt. He didn't care much for people these days. A cold shift occurred over the last decade; society had become meaner, desensitized, and disgusted by his existence on the streets, so he looked for refuge in desolate places that ordinary people were too afraid to explore.

Draped in an oversized sweater, holes and cigarette burns peppering the wool fabric, Gary sauntered forward, breathing in the crisp air. A beige hood spilled out of the neckline, stained with a number of liquids and splotches of once vibrant paint. Faded blue jeans covered his lower half, hugging his thin legs. He walked for ten miles, dragging a piece of ratty luggage behind him, wheels skidding on their last leg, smeared with filth, mud, and dead grass. His bare feet moved forward, shuffling across the cold road, but his feet felt like separate appendages.

Hard and calloused.

They rarely felt much of anything besides dull sensations. The cold asphalt eventually turned into a dirt road that led to an old farm.

An old gnarled wooden sign was planted on the side of a rotting fence, saying FOR SALE in bright red letters. Gary shivered, and the cold slithered inside the gaping holes of the remnants of the faux leather coat wrapped around his thin frame. He pulled out an expired granola bar and bit into it, sinking his yellowed teeth inside the combination of rolled oats, seeds, nuts, and honey. He briefly remembered another vagabond calling him snaggle tooth on account of his canines, they looked like they could rip through anything. This companion had gone missing a few years back, and this thought made his heart ache. Slowly chewing, he walked into the dying cornfield and looked up at a scarecrow towering over him.

The scarecrow sported a lopsided brown hat, black buttons for eyes, and lips scorched onto its hideous face, if you could call it that. Upon closer inspection, the burlap sack seemed to have been cut open beneath the nose and yellowed animal teeth poked out of the jute fabric. The misshapen body was constructed of branches, broken mop handles, and a wooden table leg. A bloated stomach extended outward, and Gary dreamed of the nice clothes and stuffing that might be hidden inside. He poked the plaid shirt with his soiled index finger, imagining warm clothes clumped together in a thick ball, clothes that could help him get through the cold months, clothes that he *needed*.

Gary looked around the barren property for covert cameras, paranoid that he was being watched and secretly filmed and wondered what happened to the owners. He figured thick cornstalks and tomatoes should be growing at this time of year, but the owners obviously fell on some hard times. The thought of fresh food made his stomach rumble and his head hurt.

Curiosity and desperation drove him to take out his pocketknife. He wished he owned a knife sharpener to offset the dullness, but he said fuck it and gutted the scarecrow with quick aggressive stabs. A foul stench erupted from the gaping holes and pink fluid oozed out. He almost vomited, taking in the smell, but breathed through it. For a moment, he questioned his sanity and thought this might be a delusion creeping up on him.

T-that can't be a wound. It's just a scarecrow. An ugly fucking scarecrow...you're in reality, Gary. You're sober and you're here in a cornfield. Everything's alright.

After composing himself, Gary slashed the fabric in wide gaping strokes so he could get a better look.

Gary had seen some atrocities in his time, being homeless and spending so much time on the streets, roaming from city to town to village to off-grid communities and the like, but what he witnessed made him feel a great sense of unease, flowering in the pit of his stomach.

Lying at his feet was a pungent mixture of pig ears, tan human hands with weird markings carved into the dead flesh, intestines, and a heart that he hoped belonged to an animal. Not a single piece of clothing came out. Disappointment, shock, and confusion burrowed into the legion of wrinkles adorning Gary's hardened face.

He wasn't the superstitious type and felt like God had deserted him long ago, but in this moment, Gary knew he fucked up. There was no tangible proof outside of the gnawing sense of unease slowly blooming into paranoia, and the wet parts on the ground steaming in the cold air. Still, the old Gary would have dropped to his knees and prayed, but he knew the gesture was worthless. God didn't care for his kind of people. He was on his own.

Gary noticed two other scarecrows in the field, but they seemed to have been damaged from his point of view, looking like a shadow of their former selves. He wondered if this small farm needed much protection from crows and animals, but he tossed the thought aside when he noticed the sun dipping beneath the horizon. It was time to find shelter, and rest his weary bones.

The barn's wooden doors whined as he opened them. The sound of horses neighing made him pause, waiting for an angry owner to come out of the darkness with a gun in hand. After some time passed and no one came to inspect the noise, the tension in Gary's stomach loosened, and he moved inside, covering his nose from the abhorrent smell of manure combined with the foul odor of animals. The overwhelming stench seemed to be imprinted into the space, bleeding into the hickory planks and ancient walls.

Suppressing a wet cough, Gary surveyed the barn, taking in the aged hay, rusted machinery, elongated shadows, and a wooden ladder that led to the second floor. He ignored the collective eye of the horses who snorted in their enclosures, watching him make his way to the ladder. Something about their frames seemed emaciated and underfed, reminding him of his mounting hunger, but instead of feeling kinship, he felt dread.

What if they think I'm a food? A nice bite to eat.

Gary had taken a few free books from one of those little libraries in the shape of a birdhouse and had read that horses were primarily herbivores, but were opportunistic carnivores, especially when they lacked certain nutrients. He eyed the locks on their gates and they seemed hefty and intact.

Letting out a sigh of relief, he climbed the ladder, feeling good about putting distance between himself and the animals, pushing away the fear of their absurdly large teeth sinking into his flesh. The wood *creaked*, making him shudder, the rungs struggling to hold the weight of his body. Sweat dripped down his back as he continued climbing until he vaulted himself over the edge. Feeling the safety of the second floor, he wiped the sweat from his forehead with his sleeve.

What a relief.

Dusting himself off, Gary stood, appraising his surroundings. The first thing that caught his eye was an old pitchfork in the corner that looked like it had been around for centuries. He ran his finger along a steel tine, noticing a weird substance that resembled blood or maybe rust smeared on his index finger.

"Nasty shit," he mumbled, yearning for hot water and soap. Little things he took for granted back when life was better, back when he had a routine and stability. Sometimes, the mundane could be the best thing a man could ask for.

Look at you now, Gary.

A ton of hay covered the floor and Gary figured this spot by the window would do for the night. Digging into his luggage, he pulled out a stained blanket and carefully unrolled it on the ground. Lying down on his side, his limbs cracked, and he ignored the pain, the body's signal that everything was wrong and out of alignment.

Gary listened to the wind howl outside the barn, thankful the horses had calmed down. He struggled to sleep due to the noise and the cold snaking its way into his clothes. He sat up, collected trash and made a small fire from the riffraff he could find. Lying back down, he fell asleep to the sound of the crackling fire, dreaming of a medium rare steak and a bowl of hot steaming soup.

Bucketfuls of soup.

Gary woke in darkness with the faint taste of cheddar broccoli on his dry tongue. He turned over, wanting to return to the warmth of his dreams, the deep satiation he found inside those porcelain bowls, but something had cracked open the barn doors even wider than before.

Moonlight spilled in, and by the time Gary could look down, he saw the feline outline of animals slipping inside. The horses blew air out of their nostrils, much more intensely than when he'd entered the space. Something about the dark shapes made Gary think about mountain lions or cheetahs the way they slinked, but it didn't make sense for these creatures to exist in Wisconsin of all places.

He'd heard of extraordinary instances of animals traveling to environments outside their normal habitat, but had never seen it with his own eyes. The prospect made his heart race, and fear took hold of him.

Maybe he could better see the animals from his vantage point if he could reposition himself and see what he was truly dealing with. Sometimes he'd overreact to situations in the past, thinking things were a bigger threat than they actually were. He shimmied to the edge on his hands and knees, feeling goosebumps form on his skin as he looked down into the darkness. He could hear them snorting and hissing below.

Gary wished he owned a Polaroid camera so he could capture this moment, but this wish washed away the moment he felt the ladder shake with the weight of a body beginning its ascent.

Creaking.

Something about this spooked him. He didn't think big cats could climb, but maybe this was a local species he wasn't familiar with. Plus, new animals were being discovered all of the time. He'd dealt with a spectrum of humans, but animals were something else. Rats, raccoons, and insects tended to be annoying neighbors when he slept in alleyways, but big cats were completely out of his element.

Feeling the desperate need for protection or some sort of security, Gary crept behind a large wheelbarrow with a flat tire, keeping his eye on the pitchfork from earlier. His knees popped as he bent down, and he hoped the sound wasn't loud enough for the felines to hear, potentially giving away his location. He slowed his breath and heard padded steps in the darkness. The pocketknife could be an option, but he doubted the thing would do enough damage.

The moonlight showed something that resembled a slim woman with red fur coating her body and pointed ears with whiskers on her face standing on her hind legs. The cat creature sniffed the air and moved in his direction. Another cat creature appeared on the floor and the two moved towards one another.

This one was somewhat taller and possessed more of an athletic frame and slightly more weight. It licked the other one's neck, and Gary heard a soft purr that almost sounded like a moan.

Must be grooming each other...

The original cat turned over on her back while the athletic one licked her pointed ear, moving down to her neck, and then her breast, circling the brown nipples. The purrs grew louder, more erotic in nature, and Gary's eyes looked downward to the thing's *wet* vagina. Blood rushed down to his groin and his cock throbbed against his jeans.

Gary couldn't remember the last time he had sex, let alone masturbated. The memories were blurred by excessive drug use and alcohol. Dim images from his early 20s, when he was healthier and better looking, rose and his cock grew even harder. He slowly unzipped his pants and pulled it out, slowly stroking. Suppressing his moans, he watched in eager anticipation as the creatures continued licking each other's bodies. He couldn't keep his eyes off the one's damp vagina, hypnotized by the wet flower, nearly forgetting the threatening aspects of the creatures.

His stroking grew more intense, and he leaned against the wheelbarrow, sweat running down his neck. His free hand leaned on the wheelbarrow and his sweaty palm slid ever so slightly, making a squeegee-like sound, going off like a crack of thunder inside his head. His cock softened a bit, but he still maintained a solid erection.

The cats moved towards the wheelbarrow and Gary's internal alarms screamed. They trilled, making him wonder what messages were being communicated between the two felines. These thoughts melted away the moment the wheelbarrow went flying, landing in a pile of hay, exposing Gary. He had no idea these cats possessed such strength based on how small they were. It didn't make sense.

What the fuck are these things? Animals or some sort of genetic experiment created on a military base?

The original cat creature approached Gary calmly and eyed his cock, licking its lips. She moved closer and ran its long tongue over his neck and then moved downwards, cleaning the dirt off his hand and then she kissed the head of his rancid cock. He moaned in ecstasy while she took the entirety of his cock inside her mouth, not caring about his putrid body odor or the warts covering his shaft.

The word bestiality came to mind and Gary's cheeks grew red with embarrassment and shame. He wasn't one of *those types* of people—degenerates and perverts. That wasn't his pedigree. He struggled with this train of thought and what people would think about him as his lust overpowered any principles left inside his rapidly beating heart. He thrust into the cat's mouth, hands sinking beneath the fur covering her head, feeling the back of her throat.

His breath hitched, and he'd almost forgotten how good it was to get head. How a woman's touch felt, the sweet ecstasy of being wanted.

The other cat watched with a strange expression on her face, and Gary wondered if he was dreaming. This seemed so surreal, but he was so hard and the creatures smelled like black cherries, pine trees, and damp earth. The smell brought him back to reality and he still struggled to accept the events unfolding.

The creature stopped, sensing Gary's fear, stood, and hunched down slowly, a furry hand wrapped around his shaft. She eased it inside her wet vagina and Gary felt as if he was transported to heaven, feeling her walls tighten around his cock. He thrust inside her, imagining her as a hot red head instead of a furry cat woman.

Her other furry hand crawled under his shirt and rested on his stomach, a claw tickling the inside of his belly button. The placement bothered him, but he continued fucking her, enjoying the moment, forgetting about his troubles, forgetting about his homelessness, forgetting about the cold and the persistent loneliness that followed him everywhere he traveled.

The cat purred with pleasure and Gary felt a soft pressure inside his stomach. A single claw punctured his belly button and sharply slashed downward. He gasped as he watched a waterfall of red blood paint his cock. Her free hand pulled him in deeper, and as he dismounted, the claw ripped through his shaft, slicing his penis in half. It split open like a banana, blood gushing outwards along with a white spray of cum.

The pain was so explosive Gary nearly left his body and blacked out. He pushed a hand over the wound in his stomach, applying as much pressure as he could, not wanting to think about the amount of blood loss he already experienced.

"Y-you bitch!" Gary yelled, pointed at her with a shaky hand. He strode towards the pitchfork, wanting revenge. Hot pain and anger mixed inside his mind. Blood continued seeping out the wound. If he was going to die, he was going to take one of these furry cunts with him.

His hand wrapped around the wooden handle of the pitchfork, and the weight of the farm tool felt awkward at first, unwieldy. The cats growled and hissed behind him. Hefting it up, Gary finally got a good grasp on it, and he staggered back into the open, prongs pointed forward.

Both cat creatures were on all fours, muscles coiled, taking on a defensive posture. He slashed at the one who watched earlier, and she leapt back lightning fast. The one he had sex with moved toward him, with a predatorial look in its eyes that made him want to piss himself.

She jumped and Gary thrust the tool forward with all his might, pulling downward slightly. The creature shrieked, and he dropped the tool, taken aback by the high-pitched cry. His pants were completely covered in blood. Something inside his stomach was sloshing out, he thought it might be his pancreas or his small intestine. His mortality, exposed and raw, made him shiver.

This might really be it, Gary. This might be the fuckin end. What do you have to show for it?

The cat creature licked its wound, struggling to dislodge the pitchfork sticking out of its side. Gary grinned, hearing the cat whine, knowing that it too might die tonight. He strode over, growing weaker by the minute, head shiny with sweat, and a bloodied hand lazily applying pressure to the wound.

"Dumb cunt," he said, snickering. "Thought you had me."

He kicked her and she mewed, looking at him with fear. A rare moment of power flooded his senses and he thought this wouldn't be the worst way to go out. Getting his dick wet and getting revenge.

Rearing his leg back, he kicked the cat creature over the edge and he watched as she tumbled through the air and fell to the ground with a satisfying *crack*.

"Well, it looks like—"

His words were cut off by the weight of the second cat creature slamming him to the ground. The blow felt like the equivalent of three grown men tackling him. He thought that couldn't be possible, she couldn't weigh that much.

Claws slashed across his face and his vision went out in one eye. Excruciating pain racked his nervous system, the likes of which he'd never experienced before. The wooden ceiling grew fuzzy, and ribbons of skin were torn from his face, exposing muscle, burning in the moonlight.

Gary wanted to say something, cuss one last time, say fuck you to the world, but his vocal cords were ripped out, his bloodied larynx dangling above him. A flash of yellowed teeth coming down was the last thing he saw before his heart ceased beating and his brain stopped functioning and his final breath left his lungs.

2

"**P**ERSONALLY, I'VE NEVER BEEN a fan of cats. Selfish bastards. *Felines.* You feed them, take care of them, and they still want to stick their ass in the air and run off like they don't even know you. I don't need that type of energy in my life."

"Mister, are you going to buy the cheese or not?" The cashier said, scrolling through her phone as she sat on the stool behind the register. She seemed like a college student with an eyebrow piercing, bad skin, and a shock of green hair. A wide variety of cheeses exclusively made in the state of Wisconsin lined the walls behind her, along with a number of cheap knick-knacks.

The tabby cat glared as Jaylen dusted dandruff off the shoulders of his black Tom Ford suit and adjusted his sunglasses, which had left a small fleshy indentation on the bridge of his brown nose.

"My bad. Ring me up," he said, pulling a wad of cash held together by a golden money clip out of his pocket.

"So you got limburger, cupola, mango fire cheddar, hvarti, muenster, and last, but not least, the holy trinity mélange gouda," the cashier said, stuffing the items into a brown paper bag.

"Sounds good. I just hope my kids like it because they've been begging for souvenirs."

"Can I make a suggestion?"

"Go ahead."

"Maybe cheese hooks, Wisconsin wine, maple syrup, chocolate, or a foam cheese head if you're a Packers fan."

"All great ideas except the last one..." he moved in closer, leaning over the counter. He squinted at her nametag. "...Trish."

"Why is that?"

"Fuck the Packers," Jaylen grabbed the bag, did a 180-degree turn, and strolled out of the Cheese Mart, making sure to spit phlegm on the ground before walking toward his car.

The sound of rocking chairs creaking made Jaylen stop and look back at a couple of elderly people occupying the seats, eyes hidden behind bulky sunglasses.

"Hey there, son," one of them said.

"Yes, sir?" Jaylen said, trying to mind his manners despite being in a rush and somewhat irritated by the idea of being mislabeled as a Packers fan of all things.

"Come closer."

Jaylen took a few steps closer, taking in the gaping hole in the old man's throat, a red scarf barely covering the void. Pegged him as a chainsmoker, skin tougher than leather, it seemed. He'd seen pictures of these things online, attributing it to throat cancer. The old man was speaking, but Jaylen's eyes remained fixated on the fleshy crater, expecting something to crawl forth from the darkness.

Absent-mindedly, Jaylen patted his own throat, making sure his voice box was still okay, imagining the outline of a healthy larynx. Thankful, he never developed a taste for that vice. Hated the taste, the way the smell penetrated every fiber of clothing, and the smoke. Nasty all the way around.

"Are you listening, son?"

"Oh sorry, could you repeat that?"

The old man's hand shot out, gripping Jaylen's wrist with his old man strength.

"Be careful around these parts, and stay off the rural roads at night."

"Why?"

Jaylen wondered if this was because of his skin color. Maybe deranged racists lived in these parts? He traveled all across the U.S., selling real estate and nothing gave him the sense that this was a no-fly zone for black people. Matter of fact, people seemed friendly, greeting him and giving him nods at different

places, and he'd seen enough diversity to make him
feel safe even at night.

"There are dangerous *things* out there, especially
in the woods. I know you young folks don't believe
in the supernatural, but there are things that would
make you piss yourself and believe in a higher power
again. Do you understand?"

"Understood."

The old man released his vice grip, and Jaylen
rubbed his own wrist, massaging the tense muscles.

*Boomer must have dementia or something. This town
is like any other town and as far as I can tell, there's
nothing special here except for that farm and the money
that comes with it.*

Supernatural, my ass.

Jaylen didn't believe in that nonsense and as a
matter of fact, the only thing he believed in was
family and the power of the dollar. That's what drove
him to hop on red-eye flights on his boss' dime and
come to shitholes in the middle of nowhere like this.

Jaylen slid into the driver's seat of his ruby red
Jaguar F-Type Convertible and tossed the bag of
cheese in the back. If he even had a single bite, he'd
have to go running to the nearest bathroom and turn
it into a nuclear wasteland. He wasn't sure how this
hellish gene of his didn't get passed down to either
of his children.

He put the car in reverse, pulled out, and skirted out of the parking lot. Jabbing in the address of the farm he was tasked with selling, he looked up at the darkening sky and wished he'd left earlier instead of subjecting himself to a marathon of video calls and meetings.

One of Jaylen's goals for the year was to make 200k off commissions alone. That was achievable if he could pull off this farm sale, which he was confident he could do, but he had some doubt that the people in this area would have enough funds to fork over.

The Hollis couple seemed desperate to sell their farm based off their communication thus far and that made Jaylen's job that much easier. In his line of work, he realized people had a tendency to hold onto things that they'd grown attached to, but the longer you held on, the more likely those things that once brought you comfort would break in time.

Jaylen was willing to break the hand all the way if necessary, especially if that brought him one step closer to that 200k commission.

3

"DID YOU GET RID of the bodies?" Barbara asked her husband. A soap opera blared on the TV screen, the sound turned up to extreme levels unbeknownst to her. At 85 years of age, her hearing had gone down the shoot, but she still had a good amount of mobility and lived with the love of her life.

That was more than enough for her.

Farm life hardened her hands and body, a quilt of wrinkles, liver spots, and sagging skin covered her exposed face and neck, but she didn't mind it. A brown blunt bob with shocks of grey hair hung down to her jawline, she took great pride in maintaining the hairstyle, cutting her own hair once a month.

Barbara embraced old age, surprised she had lived this long despite the polluted airways and dreaded chemicals that seemed to seep their way into everything. Whenever people asked how she made it this far, she attributed her longevity to quality produce grown with her own hands, not that GMO bullshit, daily walks, and an all-encompassing love.

Despite the enjoyment of farm life, she couldn't wait to have the property sold and get a fresh start. Her and her husband were getting up there in age, and couldn't work at the same pace they used to. Time had caught up to them and the toil had taken a toll, slowing them both down considerably. The farm was beginning to fall apart, the wood literally rotting, the animals seemed to need so much care, and the money was beginning to dry up.

It was time for a change.

"What did you say?" Tobias asked.

"Did you get rid of the bodies?" Barbara asked again.

"Of course, my lily flower," he said, washing his rough hands in the kitchen. She could almost smell the lavender soap gathering in the sink.

Tobias Hollis wasn't the most emotionally expressive man, but his love for Barbara emanated from his actions and consistency. Barbara thought he was a closed-off individual when she'd first met him in her 20s. However, after getting to know him, she realized he was like an onion that began to expose the innermost layers to her. And this gave her a sense of ease and safety.

"The realtor should be here any minute now," Barbara said, adjusting her posture to relieve the throbbing pain in her back. Doctors said it was due to a lack of stretching, and the tissue had calcified into something resembling a rock. You live and you learn, she told herself. "Glad you took care of that body. I know how much you detest the whole process."

"You're welcome," Tobias said, crunching on a piece of a cut-up carrot. "Sure you want to go through with this, selling the farm?"

"Yeah, I'm sure. Thought about it long and hard. And I'm looking forward to moving to Honolulu, sitting on the beach and enjoying the waves."

Tobias nodded, finishing the last of his carrot, a man with a tremendous appetite. She was surprised he hadn't cut up more, considering the work he did, dragging the cryptid out of the old barn and the disposal.

They didn't have kids or much family at all, a choice made on her end. For whatever reason, doctors said her body might not be able to withstand going into labor and that she might not make it. It was a hard decision, but one that seemed sound. Tobias was a strong man, but she didn't think his heart could take the impact of losing her.

The sound of a car pulling into the gravel driveway disturbed Barbara and Tobias departed into the kitchen to put his bowl away.

When Tobias opened the front door, the real estate agent stood there, texting on his cellphone. Barbara came up behind Tobias, detesting the devices. She owned one, out of necessity, but rarely used the damn thing.

"Hi, Mr. and Mrs. Hollis, I'm Jaylen," Jaylen said, looking up from his phone. He shook both their hands and flashed his veneers at them, grinning. Jaylen was a handsome black man dressed in an expensive suit, reeking of money, eyes hidden behind fancy sunglasses. Everything about him screamed business and excess. She wasn't sure if she could trust him, considering she couldn't see his eyes to gauge him on deeper levels.

"Would you like some lemonade?" Barbara asked, wanting to feel him out.

"Sure, I would love some," Jaylen said. "I am feeling parched."

Jaylen came in, the scent of a heady cologne making her head swim. She gripped the edge of the couch for stability. Tobias put a steady arm around her shoulders, her literal rock whenever she needed one most.

"You okay?" Jaylen asked, lowering his sunglasses, concern painted across his face.

"She's fine," Tobias said in a gruff tone.

Jaylen followed them to the kitchen, folding his sunglasses and putting them into his pocket. He scanned the room, appraising the square footage, the cabinetry, the floors, the ceilings, the furniture, the paintings, their photos, and the old stove. Barbara wondered what he saw when he looked at their home.

Does he see the true value or an ugliness concealed inside these walls?

"How do you like the place?" Tobias asked, almost reading Barbara's mind. She always felt like they had an uncanny connection, one that was much more than flesh and blood, bordering on the telepathic.

"It's lovely," Jaylen said. "The salesman in me would use words like rustic and cozy to describe the aesthetics, which is appealing in today's market. People have a desire to return to simpler times, and get away from the chaos of city life. If you're wondering if it will sell, I bet every dollar in my bank account on it."

Barbara beamed at this comment, "Oh gosh, thank you for the kind words. We have so many memories here. I just hope the new owners will treat it with care."

Jaylen paused for a moment, sipping on the lemonade. The beverage sloshed around the glass and the ice cubes *clinked* against one another. "This is great by the way, homemade?"

"Why of course," Barbara said, thinking back to the organic lemons she bought from another farmer every third Saturday of the month. She respected his efforts to remineralise the soil on his property. Tobias started adding rock dust to their own land about five years back and the difference in crops was astounding.

"I'm sure we'll find someone who will love to call this place home and treat it like a child."

"Well if this place is a child, it's deep into adulthood and could be moving into middle age at this point," Barbara quipped.

The three of them chuckled.

"How about we head outside so you can get a full tour of the property?" Tobias asked, finishing off his glass of lemonade.

"Lead the way," Jaylen said. "You don't mind if I bring this glass with me?"

"Not at all," Tobias said, giving Barbara a weak smile. He wasn't the most extroverted man, but he was giving it his all and that made Barbara happy. His social battery didn't last the longest, but Barbara was prepared to take the lead if it ran out.

"Excuse my language, but these are some ugly motherfuckers," Jaylen said.

"They're not the most flattering, but they're effective," Barbara said, looking at the scarecrows that still needed to be fixed and remodeled.

"Really?" Jaylen asked, plucking a piece of straw from its stomach. "These things protect your property, they scare off birds and animals? Thought that was a myth, an old wives-tale."

"No myth," Tobias said. "We wouldn't be able to sell this property if these didn't exist. They're essential."

"Damn, I had no idea. Always thought it was bs."

"Scarecrows go way back," Barbara said, looking at the long milky shadows running across the field. As her gaze moved to the tree line, watching the easter red cedars, bur oaks, and black spruces sway in the wind, a chill ran down her neck and she wished she had brought a coat outside to keep her warm. "The Egyptians hung tunics on reeds and used wooden frames covered with nets to scare quails from their crops. The Greeks and Romans put up wooden figures that resembled the god of fertility. I can't recall the name, but it kept birds away from gardens and vineyards. Native Americans would just put dead birds on poles and that seemed to do the trick."

"Wow," Jaylen said, a genuineness in his voice that made Barbara feel like she didn't waste her breath. "Thank you for that history lesson."

"You're welcome. A lot of farmers have done away with scarecrows, going with noise machines, automated systems, and the like. Technology can't replace these," Barbara said, patting the bloated stomach of a scarecrow towering over them. "What has worked for centuries, has worked for good reason. Foolish to do away with something so important."

Tobias moved by Barbara's side, softly rubbing her back. "I pray the next owners don't do away with the scarecrows. Please tell them. Will you do that for us? It's essential to this particular farm's livelihood."

"Yeah, you have my word," Jaylen said, nodding. "But why, what will happen if they don't listen? I mean I can pass on the message, but I can't guarantee they'll listen. You know how people are."

Tobias clamped a heavy hand on Jaylen's shoulder and squeezed. The realtor let out a small noise, surprised by the man's strength and the serious energy exuding from the old farmer. "Heartache, pain, and loss. The kind of woes that don't pass with time, but grow and spread like a weed."

4

T HE OLD COUPLE, COMBINED with the sight of the grotesque scarecrows, gave Jaylen the creeps. Normally, he loved every minute of his job, almost every minute, but the time spent on the Hollis property felt like an extended outtake from *The Twilight Zone*. The couple moved extremely slow, and something about the soft tone of Barbara's voice made his muscles feel tired and his eyelids grow heavy. He considered driving up the road, adjusting his car seat back, kicking his feet up, and catching a few z's.

Despite his tiredness and desire for sleep, Jaylen passed on the idea. He didn't know these parts well, and the old man's words outside the cheese shop spooked him. What if there were some rabid animals he didn't know about that were native to Wisconsin? He wasn't going to fuck around and find out. The hotel would have to do, and Jaylen wasn't one to play with fire or to test the temperature of unknown dangers.

As Jaylen cruised back to the hotel, he made a few phone calls to potential buyers to see if he could set up tour times. The farm was a bit of a shithole and desperately needed a remodel, but people would still buy it. What he told the couple wasn't dishonest in the slightest. He would reframe and sell the architectural flaws as "rustic charm and a vintage touch." There was a time Jaylen struggled to close sales despite having charisma and a quick tongue, but there was something missing.

So, he studied Edward Bernays and learned that people acted on unconscious desires and group psychology rather than logic.

Jaylen sold dreams and these homes were the perfect vessel to house these desires. People fell for buzzwords that were associated with prestige, new identities, and social proof as long as you said it with your chest and polished the delivery with a warm smile.

Hook. Line and sinker.

Jaylen's left shoulder ached with pain, and he wondered why the old man squeezed it so hard. Thick fingers felt like they were constructed from rocks instead of skin and flesh. Didn't realize being a farmer could turn your hands into basalt.

He massaged his shoulder with his hand, and attempted to work the pain out, but it didn't do much. Wished he could book a massage to remedy this issue, but he didn't have faith the locals could get the job done. This was one of those moments he missed being back home in Tribeca, NY, he missed his kids, and he missed his wife.

His daughter would have most likely given him a crayon drawing and his wife would have kissed the pain away. And if that didn't work, he'd book a Swedish massage at the Four Seasons hotel with heated lava rocks. That did the trick every time the tension and knots built up in his body and he needed to reset.

He thought back to the old man's words, how he brought up death and gendered it *she*.

Probably just fucking with you, he thought, but the man seemed dead serious. And the scarecrows were repulsive, something about the hay effigies seemed different than any he'd come across in his youth. Most of them were ugly but charming in a sense. Yet these made his stomach hurt just thinking about them, and a strange, disconcerting energy waded off the hay men in waves.

They were much uglier and cruder than anything he'd seen on any farm. Their bodies seemed misshapen and ill-proportioned as if they were housing something more wicked than hay. He couldn't put his finger on it, a part of him thinking he was being paranoid, but it was hard to erase them from his mind no matter how hard he focused on visualizing the sale.

Just as he pulled into the hotel parking lot, his phone went off. It gave him a start, heart racing, and he took a deep breath to calm his nerves. He didn't realize how deeply he had sunk into the muck of his thoughts, his body going into autopilot as he drove the car back. Visceral images of those scarecrows burned into his mind like ancient totems, the crop watchers were hard to shake from his mental soil, firmly rooted in his psyche.

The phone continued ringing. His wife's name Nala displayed on the screen along with a couple of pink heart emojis. He tapped accept and put the phone on speaker mode.

"Daddy, I miss you," Amara said, the sadness heavy and present in her voice.

Jaylen's heart felt as if a giant was squeezing the organ. Nothing compared to the depth of his love for his daughters, not even this farm sale or the money he had amassed over the years.

"I miss you too," Jaylen said.

"When are you coming home, daddy?" his oldest Simone asked.

Jaylen grinned, hearing the familiar tones and textures, momentarily feeling light again. Once he looked at the sun hovering above the horizon, he took a moment contemplating the answer and the ease turned into dread. He didn't know when he'd be home and that answer made his head hurt.

Still, he needed to make that sale. He'd been a top seller in the company for the last decade, but this year he wanted to take it to the next level. That bastard Bryce Harlow was his sole competition, the man edging him out as real estate agent of the year. If he could get that 200k commission, he'd snatch that title from Bryce's hands and also get the mystery bonus that came with it.

"Daddy, you still there?" Simone asked.

"Yeah, sorry about that," he said, clearing his throat as his car was consumed by darkness. "Daddy will be home soon."

"You sure?" his daughter asked.

"God willing."

5

TOBIAS HATED TOUCHING THE creatures, hated getting rid of the bodies, hated the strange smell wafting off their fur that tickled the inside of his nostrils and seeped into the fibers of his clothes, but what he hated most of all, *loathed* was a better word, was putting up the scarecrows. Taking the limp bodies and placing them on the tall poles overlooking the fields wasn't too bad. The occult ritual on the other hand, made him queasy and gave him a severe sense of unease.

When he inherited the farm from his folks, he had no idea it would be such a pain in the ass to maintain. Sure, he knew farming was a lot of hard work, manual labor, and the like, but the occult aspects weren't something he signed up for.

The instructions for maintaining the farm had been buried inside an old mahogany chest sitting at the foot of the king-size bed in the master bedroom. Tobias managed to break the rusted lock with a hammer. The lid whined open, and the dust gave him a coughing fit. He found old photos of his parents, a dead rat, flesh eaten away by the passage of time and maggots, and leatherbound books. Flipping through the large tome, Tobias skimmed through long passages and dark images, written in red ink, describing the cat creatures in the woods and the scarecrows that kept them at bay. These weren't any scarecrows, though; these scarecrows had to have trinkets, animal parts, and other personal items stuffed inside. And strange words spoken over them.

Spells.

It took Tobias some convincing, but not too much. Barbara wasn't sure what to make of them, and Tobias thought these writings had to be folklore, local rubbish penned by the hands of someone with an overactive imagination and too much idle time. His parents were far from creative and he couldn't see them reading anything so fantastical for fun.

The *Farmers' Almanac*, the *Ball Complete Book of Home Preserving*, coffee-stained guides on machinery repairs, crops, and animal husbandry were the only books Tobias could remember seeing them consume on a regular basis.

The cat creatures came on the seventh night. Tobias woke to the sound of the horses baying as he wiped the drool coating his beard. He'd never heard his steeds sound so frightened before, they usually gave him no problems at night, none of his animals did. This anomaly put his nerves on edge as he quickly laced his work boots and grabbed the shotgun off the mantle.

The stable resembled a slaughterhouse rather than a home for the horses. When Tobias stepped inside, the air smelled like iron and musk rather than manure, urine, and hay. He forbade Barbara from walking in, knowing the sight would traumatize her. He wasn't sure if he had the stomach for it. She wanted to come in, worried about the animals, but when she saw the haunted look on Tobias' face, she listened. Shit, Tobias had seen some grim sights in his time, but this made his skin crawl and shook his faith in a higher power.

Exploring his property with a large flashlight, and shotgun, he saw one of the bitches licking blood off its paws in the cornfield. He killed *it* underneath the moonlight, taking it out with a headshot. This act made the others hidden in the shadows scurry off into the woods. Tobias attempted to follow them to the edge of his property line, but knew it would be too dangerous to go deep into the woods at such a later hour. He might as well have a death wish.

Prior to this, he'd been no stranger to taking out animals. He'd killed several coyotes, hawks, and put down livestock that had grown sick or had been injured. This was different though. These animals moved with a frightening speed and ferocity, and resembled women.

Human women with catlike features. Had to be the devil's work. He'd been taught by his old man to treat women with the utmost respect and never to raise a hand. So the killing act made him feel guilty for shooting the bitch even though it had shown his horses no mercy. The cat creatures had a beguiling quality about them and they seduced him inside his dreams and outside his home for the next couple weeks.

Tobias would wake in the middle of the night, hearing a series of meows outside his bedroom window. Barbara turned towards Tobias, snoring softly. He thought it was cute, not wanting to bother her, he planted a wet kiss on her forehead.

The meows started back up, pulling his attention away from his wife. He tried ignoring them, but they became more insistent with a slight sensual edge.

Feeling crazy and curious, he wanted to investigate the sound, almost feeling called to step outside. He carefully walked downstairs, laced his workboots, threw on a warm coat, and thought about grabbing his shotgun.

Don't be a pussy, it's just a bunch of cats, he told himself, doing his best to get rid of his fears.

He stepped outside with a flashlight in hand, eyes taking a moment to adjust to the darkness. Scanning the earth with his flashlight, he couldn't find a single stray cat and thought about turning back inside. When his hand grabbed the doorknob, something warm and soft brushed up against his body, a woman's touch.

"Ma'am—"

His words were cut short when he turned around and saw a trio of cat women with red fur, standing with their hands on their hips. Sexual energy dripped off their feline frames and Tobias had a hard time keeping his eyes off their curves. His manhood grew inside his trousers and he was surprised he didn't feel an ounce of fear.

He knew they were dangerous and could rip him to shreds, but his amygdala felt numb. They purred seductively, one sauntering over and pressing her vagina against his groin. It was soaking wet and his cock grew harder. She licked his neck, sliding her paw inside his trouser, wrapping her warm hand around his shaft, stroking him.

Tobias moaned, feeling like this was wrong on so many levels, but not wanting it to end. He hadn't experienced pleasure like this in ages. The cat woman purred louder and pulled his cock out into the cold air. He was surprised it still worked as she rubbed her rump against it, tail swaying back and forth. Failing to hold himself back, he came, white fluid consumed by the soil.

The sexual act made him come to his senses for a moment and he shoved the cat woman back. She hissed. He turned the doorknob and ran back inside.

A heavy *thump* followed and a series of loud agitated purrs. Sweating, he thought about grabbing his gun, but wasn't sure if he could resist his sexual urges.

He considered waking Barbara and confessing to the blasphemous act he just engaged in, but felt too ashamed. The cats continued coming at night, but he managed to keep himself in check and ignore their enchantments.

Several passages in the old books had warned him against these cat creatures. They had a name, but that piece of writing was illegible, ink faded with time, and he wasn't willing to travel somewhere ridiculous to get a writing expert to decipher the words.

Before taking over the land, Tobias thought magic was fake, simply stage tricks and illusions, but he quickly learned that the crops grew plentiful, and the land was safe as long as he and his lovely wife Barbara properly maintained them. The only magic he ever experienced before this was the wonders of love, sharing a nice meal he grew with his own hands, and enjoying the stunning beauty of a sunset.

These sunsets became anxiety-inducing moments overtime after a cold winter storm blew in and tore the scarecrows apart. He figured the cat creatures took refuge in a warm cave or migrated somewhere warmer during the winter months. They came out of hiding and tore apart the horses. The whines in the stable still haunted Tobias and ravaged his dreams.

Jaylen seemed like a city boy concerned with money and expensive clothes, but he was nice enough and kind to Barbara. That was enough for Tobias, but would he listen and pass along the message? He didn't want the new owners to become caught off guard and traumatized with fresh horrors. Maybe he'd firmly press the request again when it was time to sign the last of the paperwork.

Tobias sighed, knowing the truth would be far too ridiculous and too much for the real estate agent to bear.

6

WHEN EBONY CHAMBERS TOOK the job, she
had no idea the wealthy French woman would
send her to a muddy cornfield, in the middle of
Wisconsin, of all places. However, she had grown
accustomed to being sent to a wide range of
destinations like Coahuila, the Congo River basin,
the Pacific Northwest, the Banksia Swamp, and more.
Wisconsin was not on her bucket list, but the money
was good combined with the love of the cryptid hunt
and her need for the rush of adrenaline brought her
here.

Ebony cracked her neck, followed by her knuckles
before stepping outside of her truck. Her body was
always stiff and coiled with tension despite daily
stretches, a well-used massage gun, foam rollers, a
cryotherapy membership, and Thai massages. She
thought it was just the way she was wired, while her
therapist informed her that the body kept the score
and this was due to years of trauma entrenched in her
physicality. A brand new hardcover edition of the book

The Body Keeps the Score was somewhere in her trunk, hidden underneath a mini armory of weapons.

I'll get to it eventually. The hunt is top priority at the moment. My trauma will have to wait.

Whenever Ebony was on a job, she kept her full focus on the hunt. Distractions and daydreams got multiple colleagues and competitors killed. She knew her field of work was highly dangerous, but that's what also made it exhilarating.

During her stint in the Navy, adrenaline became a part of the job, but something she needed and craved overtime. Her brothers in arms called her an adrenaline junkie and they weren't lying. She'd get her fix during combat missions, but when she left, the transition was hard due to the lack of action and the gaping void it left. Hunting cryptids scratched this itch in ways she could only dream of.

Her employer, Emma-Delphine Tautou, contacted her three months ago, through an encrypted communication system Ebony had set up when she first established her business. The proper code words were said along with a detailed itinerary and a hotel room booking. The next day, she was flown out first class to the dirty streets of Paris and strolled into the Hotel Parc Saint-Severin- Espirit de France. A black Peugeot 508 PSE pulled up and a chauffeur built like a California bear sporting a military cut, an expensive earpiece, and a fitted black suit, opened the door for Ebony.

"Get in, madam," he said with a thick accent.

Ebony thought about 20 different ways she could kill him in case things went South. She was a black woman in a foreign country going to meet French wealth about hunting cryptids—anything could happen.

Ebony expected to pull up to a private townhouse, a lofty flat or a luxury penthouse. Instead, she found herself standing in front of a Haussmannian Apartment. There was a charm to the cream colored Lutetian stone, large windows, steeply sloped mansard roofs, and wrought-iron balconies. The chauffeur led her into the interior, where she looked in awe at the high ceilings, parquet floors, and ornate molding.

"This place is so beautiful," Ebony said in awe, taking it all in. Part of her enjoyed architecture and the history that came with it.

"It truly is," Tatou said, making a grand entrance with a large glass of champagne clutched between two olive-toned hands adorned in chunky pieces of gold jewelry.

Tautou spoke in a thick yet soft French accent and seemed to float everywhere she walked, despite walking in expensive heels. She wore a long vermilion dress that hugged her tall, lithe frame and gaudy jewelry that shone even in the darkness. Her face consisted of sharp angles, severe features and a pointed chin, a blighted element that had spread downward to her shoulders and clavicles, possessing the ability to cut anyone who got too close even in the cradle of a warm embrace.

Ebony had a good sense for feeling out threats and this woman had her internal alarms going crazy. She moved cautiously around Tautou and watched her words. This suspicion was confirmed when Tautou guided her into a secret room hidden behind a bookshelf in her elaborate library.

"Welcome to the Galerie," Tatou said, spinning in a dramatic circle, gesturing towards several animal heads mounted on the wall. A manic sasquatch glared at Ebony while half of a chupacabra's body hung down, razor-sharp claws polished to the point you almost forgot they could rip through your flesh along with several other heads that were hard to label and categorize. Shadowy creatures floated in sticky pools of amber that resembled exotic statues while disembodied animal parts rotated on automated circular showpiece tables.

"Quite astonishing, I know."

"Whoever you hired to acquire these…must have been pretty talented," Ebony said, flipping through a mental Rolodex of peers and competitors. "Respected in the field."

"The last two hunters were fantastic. Real serious men. One was taken by Father Time, arthritis settling into his joints like a witch's curse. Says he was retiring somewhere warm. Tropical."

"The other?"

"Well, he died on the very job I'm hiring you to complete. And before you ask more questions, just know your reputation precedes you, Ebony Chambers. You will be handsomely rewarded for your time and expertise."

Ebony nodded, wondering how Tatou made her fortune and sustained her wealth. She wasn't on any Forbes list or world's wealthiest family document, she was one of those people who moved in the shadows, preferring to stay out of the limelight. Ebony respected that quality despite the fact that the two of them came from vastly different worlds and cultural backgrounds. Everyone didn't deserve to know everything about you; some things were meant to be private and kept sacred.

Ebony had no idea what these cryptids were called. Their original names were either lost to the passage of time or were notated in an old dusty book. The profile that was sent over said they had humanoid features and red fur combined with feline characteristics. Details were vague and sparse, but that didn't stop her from accepting the job.

She kept her eyes focused on the dense tree line and scanned the area for life with her infrared goggles.

Nothing yet.

The only thing popping up in her field of vision was the two red splotches walking inside the single house on the property. She researched the owners, an old couple who lived on this land for the last 50 years. Tobias and Barbara Hollis were quiet for the most part, but Ebony gasped when she saw Tobias dragging a feline body out into the field.

Despite his age, he possessed that mythical old man strength, dusting himself off after dropping the body into a makeshift ditch. He disappeared into the barn and came back pushing a wheelbarrow, full of chopped wood, foliage, and a container of lighter fluid. Tobias threw the contents into the ditch and squeezed out a liberal amount of lighter fluid, covering everything in the liquid.

He took out a single match, lit it and tossed it into the ditch. Flames swooshed upward into the sky and Tobias took out a tobacco pipe, packing the wooden device and lighting it. He stood there, watching the flames devour the cryptid's body as a vile odor wafted toward Ebony's hiding place, reminding her of the time she was sent into the sewers of New York City for a job, but somehow this shit was so much worse. Her nose twitched, a sneeze struggling to be born inside her nostrils. She held her breath, a technique an old Marine veteran taught her back when she served, successfully extinguishing the sternutation.

She shifted her ocular setting and zoomed in on the old man. Dark shadows painted his face as he inhaled the tobacco from his pipe, and exhaled a liberal puff of smoke. A grin penetrated the darkness and Ebony wondered if she needed to keep a closer eye on this couple.

7

"YOU HAVE AN ASTONISHING 420 acres of beautiful land with a legacy farm and plenty of space for outdoor recreation. It's really a steal considering the price point."

"Can you hunt out here?" Oliver said, adjusting his sunglasses. He walked with the swagger only a man with deep pockets possessed. Jaylen knew his type from a mile away. "Looks like plenty of forest that has prime game."

"Well yes, with a hunting license of course."

"My apologies, I phrased that wrong," Oliver said. "I meant do they offer hunting on this property? They'd be making a killing if they did."

"No, they used to, but for personal reasons, they stopped."

"Hmmmm... maybe they're retarded because that's the first thing I would do if I buy this place," Oliver said, putting his hands on his hips.

"Smart man," Jaylen said, giving him a light smack on the back. People liked to be validated, and words of affirmation had a tendency of buttering prospective buyers up. All part of the game.

"I've been told that on occasion," Oliver said. "Sometimes I feel like the missus doesn't recognize my brilliance. I'm sure you can relate?"

"Yeah bro, I can."

The Swanson family seemed nice enough. There was Oliver Swanson and his wife Clara Swanson, who wandered across the property with their college-bound daughter Lily. They were most likely taking pics and enjoying the lemonade Barbara provided.

Jaylen showed Oliver around the barn, the Hollis household, and a few other spaces. He had a difficult time reading Oliver. The man seemed interested, said all the right things, but his mind seemed preoccupied, ruminating on something elsewhere. This didn't give Jaylen the best feeling and he wondered if he should consider reaching out to the other clients on his list. He was going to make this sale happen and cinch that 200k commission by any means. Took everything in him to resist the urge to start texting other clients in front of Oliver, but he was already wording the messages inside his head.

Still, this didn't take anything away from Jaylen's confidence. He was used to selling properties on the first tour and people would big him up. One Take Jay was a nickname many peers, friends, and family members called him back home in NYC on accord of him being able to sell these homes so quickly. People trusted him, his down-to-earth charm and the sense of ease that emanated from his body. It served him well and kept his bank account thick.

"Any thoughts?" Jaylen said, wanting to cut to the chase.

"Great property," Oliver said, inhaling the crisp air. "Hunting is the big selling point for me. I could care less about the crops and the farm animals."

"I understand that," Jaylen said. "Any concerns?"

"Upkeep and renovations aren't a big deal," Oliver said, throwing his hand in the air. "My only concern are these hideous fucks they have on the poles."

One of these hideous fucks wasn't too far from them. The scarecrow looked terrible as if its entire body had been desecrated. Large ragged holes dotted its stomach, and it seemed to be bloated in some spots while others seemed anorexic and thinning.

"Can't say I don't agree with you. Not the best looking guys, but aren't they supposed to be designed that way?"

"Yeah, but something about these is too ugly, too heinous. Gives me the goosebumps."

"Yeah, they do have a weird energy about them."

Oliver's wife Clara came running over, not too fast, but her stride was uneven, out of control.

"Oliver!" Clara called out.

"What's wrong?" Oliver asked.

She looked concerned, staring into the black abyss of her cellphone.

"Honey, what's wrong?" Oliver asked, moving to her side.

She was still silent.

"And where's Lily?" he asked.

"That's the problem," Clara said, hearing their daughter's name seemed to bring her back to reality and a tear ran down her cheek. "I think she went off into the woods. She's not answering her phone. What do we do? Like what the fuck do we do?"

Hearing this statement made Jaylen's stomach drop. He'd run into issues and complications in the past, but nothing of this magnitude. Sure there were rats, termites, plumbing issues, renovation and repair, missing paperwork, etc. However, this was something new, something that made him feel like that money was slipping out his hands by the minute. He'd never had someone go missing on one of his property tours and he'd seen it all or at least he thought he did.

Panic set in and his suit felt too tight, restrictive. Jaylen couldn't find the words, the words that always seemed to be there, but the endless stream seemed to have dried up and grown barren.

The sound of Clara's voice somehow made the chaos inside Jaylen's head more intense, the words themselves becoming sharpened points, cracking like a twig in the woods, fading into the clusters of trees, twisted limbs beckoning them forward.

8

LILY SNAPPED PHOTOS WITH her Fujifilm Instax matcha green camera. She enjoyed hearing the whirring of the gears inside as it spit out polaroids. Waving the black photo in the air, she waited for the captured imagery to reveal itself. She didn't consider herself an artist, but this was a fun hobby she picked up since she noticed one of her favorite content creators page layout with film photos rather than digital.

The grainy vintage style appealed to something deep inside Lily, and she wanted to connect with this feeling on a deeper level. She followed an author named Matt Cardin who always spoke about the inner daimon, and broke down ways to connect with your muse. The idea of a personal daimon or demon, scared and titillated her, imagining a tight spiky leash around the shadowy creature's neck.

It quickly turned into a hobby, and something fun, exploratory. Her classmates and peers seemed to vibe with the new pics she posted online.

A close friend of hers recently got into tarot, pulling a card for her after sharing a few photos. It depicted a goofy man in a cartoonish outfit with a weird hat, the name of the card held the perfect name for the jovial figure.

"The Fool represents new beginnings, new pathways, new doors. Lily this could be the start of a new chapter for you. Your inner child is smiling with joy as we speak."

"Really?"

"Yeah, the cards are living entities with celestial messages from the divine. Embrace this path, it'll lead to something special, something transformative. I'm so excited for you!"

Something inside Lily's gut stirred as she delved deeper into the woods, camera held tightly in her right hand. The photos were developed and she inspected them under the dimming light. The trees bent down at strange angles and she thought she spotted the silhouette of something crouching on a branch. She squinted, trying to discern the shape that didn't quite make sense. A twig snapped, breaking Lily's concentration and she wiped the sweat from her brow, looking around for the source of the sound.

Birds continued chirping, cicadas hummed, and hackleberry trees swayed in the wind. Something about these sounds gave her the creeps, making her want to head back to the farmhouse and join her boring parents, but she read somewhere that true art was on the other side of fear. So she forced herself to step even deeper into the woods, shadows wrapping around her body like a sleeve.

She snapped another photo, biting her bottom lip after hearing the shutter click echoing throughout the trees.

Stop acting like a scaredy cat, Lily. Just a bunch of trees and insects. Nothing that could hurt you or do real damage. Take a deep breath, that's right. Fear and paranoia, nothing else.

That's when the shadows darkened, a blur moved in her peripheral, and a pungent musky odor assaulted her senses. She coughed as the smell curled deep inside her nostrils and she dropped her camera. As she bent down to retrieve it, something wrapped its furry arm around her waist, the air leaving her lungs. Still, she resisted, shoving an elbow back into red fur and doing her best to escape the hold. The arm grew tighter, spittle leaving Lily's mouth and before she could yell for help, a clawed paw smothered the first decibel that wanted to escape her throat.

9

E BONY CHAMBERS WAS NAMED after her
mother's favorite color, a specific shade of dark
brown that she considered to be the most beautiful
thing in the world. Every part of Ebony lived up to
her namesake, from her dimples, to her warm smile, to
her defined cheekbones, to her slim figure, to her rich
brown eyes, to her long flowing black hair.

Beautiful.

Most people in her field laughed when she told them
she was a hunter. Grizzled men who'd spent countless
hours in all manner of terrain. She could see them
mumbling among themselves—there's no way this
pretty girl enjoyed hunting. On the contrary, she was
obsessed with hunting, fueled by passion, adrenaline,
and focus; enamored by the killing act.

Ebony unrolled her leather knife roll bag onto
her passenger seat, unveiling the small knives that
her friend Chef Hirayama had gifted her. He did
this once every five years, wanting Ebony to test
these out during her hunts. She always reported the

results back to Hirayama in detail, noting things like sharpness, durability, versatility, etc. They came in handy, especially in close combat. One couldn't rely on firearms in every scenario, best to be prepared for whatever hell throws your way.

Chef Hirayama was someone she stumbled across on a cryptid hunt in Japan. Funnily enough his namesake meant "peaceful mountain" and she'd met him at a restaurant he owned and operated in the city of the Minami-Alps, Yamanashi Prefecture, right outside the Mount Kita. The famous Japanese mountain housed a Lovecraftian cryptid, a cosmic monster that people whispered about at night.

Engaging in her pre-hunting ritual of seeking a good last meal, Ebony sought out something local and filling. This goal was accomplished when she rolled a set of dice in her head and stepped inside a random restaurant. Hirayama, a towering man, with the kindest disposition, perfected Hōtō — Yamanashi's hearty signature noodle stew. The chef used local buckwheat spring water for the handmade soba and udon. It was one of the best meals she had ever had and it gave her the fuel she needed to complete the hunt that same day.

Ebony made sure her camouflaged tent and sleeping bag was hidden on the edge of the forest, several yards from the road. She needed to make a drive into town before she went into encampment mode. As per her customary cryptid hunting ritual, she needed to get a good meal in her stomach. A pre-reward of sorts for whatever hell she was sure to face in the coming days. Plus, she knew she'd be living off Meals Ready to Eat (MRE)s and spring water depending on the length of her stay.

A realistic yet grim part of her knew that any day out here could be her last, so she thought of it as a potential last meal. She didn't like dwelling on this potential outcome, but doing it made her feel more grounded and at ease in a roundabout way.

She pulled into a diner that didn't seem too busy at the moment. 90's movie memorabilia, Green Bay Packers merch, signed jerseys, and cheese corks covered the walls. A hostess led her to a booth towards the back and she shimmied inside, making sure she could keep her eyes on the door. Sometimes these hunting expeditions attracted competitive spirits and other contractors interested in securing a huge payday.

For whatever reason, Ebony was relatively lucky in this department. She would find evidence of hunters who camped in various locales: candy wrappers, blood-smeared tracking devices, broken weapons, traps, etc. One time she was sleeping in the desert sun and woke to a knife kissing her throat. She breathed calmly, staring at a set of green eyes surrounded by pools of white. Minty breath assaulted her senses, waking her up fully, brain firing on all cylinders. But she felt no fear.

"Why are you here?"

"I'm hunting."

"That's obvious, but you do realize I have dibs on this cryptid."

"There's more than one."

"I know, but this is my space, my territory. You know the rules."

"Please direct me to the official rulebook and website for cryptid hunting."

"How can you be such a smartass with a knife to your throat?"

"Been here plenty of times."

"Maybe I should just kill you right here and dump your body in the dunes. No one would be the wiser."

Ebony sent a knee upwards and gripped his wrist, twisting it to the left. The knife fell to the ground as she rolled to the left, enclosing his lower half in her hips/thighs and leveraged their combined weight until she was atop him. He threw a jab which she dodged with ease, but the right hook grazed her lips.

She elbowed his throat, watching his breath hitch. Then she kneed his liver and karate-chopped his carotid artery. His eyes rolled into the back of his head, and she pushed him out of her tent into the desert sand, lugging him into the dunes. The sand was soft as silk, and the desert winds began blowing the grains over his body. He was buried in a matter of hours, consumed by the arid expanse.

"Rest easy."

Ebony's lemonade tasted more bitter than usual. She didn't like taking human lives if it could be avoided. Of course, she had a body count that was hazy in her mind from various military operations, but she felt like that was an unfortunate consequence of her duties and her contract. Killing cryptids, on the other hand, made her feel a sense of glee, power, and accomplishment. Most of the creatures had killed an absurd amount of humans and were highly intelligent, highly dangerous, or a combination of both.

She ripped into her steak, cutting through the tender beef with her knife, preferring it a little bloody. Surprised by the quality, tenderness, and flavor, she was glad she chose the spot. It had good reviews, and people said it was a hidden gem. They weren't lying. She thanked her intuition, knowing it served her in the strangest way at the strangest times, especially when it came to choosing restaurants.

Still, she wasn't quite sure how to feel about Rat Hollow Road, the lone street that was home to the Hollis farm and strange scarecrows. It was obvious that the couple had grown tired of maintaining the farm, but most likely tired of fighting off the cat cryptids. She was surprised they made it this long and wished she could pick their brains about it.

Thanks to experience, she had learned that it was best to initiate no contact with certain locals. Their responses and reactions were oftentimes unpredictable. She didn't feel like dealing with two spooked old people with PTSD. They might as well have been fighting in the trenches, just the agricultural kind.

Ebony figured she'd stay solo, get in and get out, take the body back to France and get paid. Should only take a couple days to accomplish as long as there were no hitches. She paid the bill and left a nice tip for the waitress and headed back with a full stomach and an appetite for hunting that needed to be wetted.

10

W*E SHOULD NEVER HAVE sold this farm.*

So many memories, so much nostalgia...so much bloodshed.

I told Tobias it was a bad idea. Hard-headed man of mine. I tried talking him out of it, convincing him to reconsider, but he wouldn't listen. Now these poor people are about to lose their daughter to the...

Barbara sniffled, restraining herself from sinking into a miasma of fear and turmoil. Instead, she thought about waking Tobias, shaking his large, muscular shoulders, but the man slept like a log at his old age. He still put in a ton of work on the farm despite her protests, taking pride in using his coarse hands and staying active. He would wake eventually, but she worried that might be too late.

Part of her thought about grabbing the shotgun off the mantle and going off into the woods by herself, but Tobias crept into her mind, scolding her.

"Don't you dare go into those woods. I can't have those wretched creatures…touch you. The end of you would be the end of me."

Her gaze fell from the shotgun and hovered over the wood planks on the floor. She knew it would be stupid to go into the forest. The voices of the wife and husband bickered back and forth. She could only imagine Jaylen's concern.

Barbara rushed into the master bedroom as fast as her old age let her. Tobias slept on his back, arms and legs splayed out. Drool coated his long grey beard, and he snored loudly.

"Tobias! Please wake up!"

He continued snoring, unaware that she was calling his name.

"Tobias, I need you. That poor family… their daughter is missing. I'm afraid something terrible is going to happen to her if we don't intervene."

Tobias groaned and turned onto his side, still snoring.

"Tobias, please!"

Barbara grabbed his hand and bent down on her aching knees, squeezing his palm with all the strength she could muster. Tobias wasn't waking up anytime soon and she felt utterly helpless. She imagined that poor girl being ripped apart by those savage abominations in the woods.

Tears ran down her sniffling cheeks and she prayed, praying that the girl would be afforded some mercy and not the painful death she imagined in her frazzled mind.

"Lily, I pray you're still alive..."

11

T HE FOOD WAS AMAZING, but for some reason, it didn't sit well in Ebony's stomach. Everything seemed fresh and tasted good. She doubted that something was spoiled or expired, but her stomach bubbled and groaned.

Something was wrong.

Is this my intuition trying to tell me something?

Ebony brought a healthy amount of skepticism to things like psychics, but she knew intuition was a real thing and it felt like it was attempting to speak to her. What could be wrong though?

She'd only been gone from camp for two hours. None of the infrared signatures moved outside of the forest since she'd been there. However, she wondered if they were aware of her presence and waited until she left. Images of her tent and supplies torn apart and ransacked plagued her mind.

These worries moved through her mind like a black cloud, almost making her forget that she was buying a souvenir. She quickly paid for a Wisconsin shot glass, feeling like that would be a worthy addition to her collection that she had amassed throughout the years.

After being rung up and rushing outside, Ebony jogged to her truck. She backed up and skirted out of the parking lot and got back on the road. She sped towards the Hollis farm, not giving a fuck about the speed limit. This could be a matter of life and death.

Every hunter wasn't the same. Some had no moral compass and didn't give a damn if innocent lives were taken. Ebony was different, she had a big heart and cared for others, sometimes too much.

The farm came into view and so did the sign saying Rat Hollow Road and part of her calmed, knowing she was about to get a handle on the situation. A couple of cars were parked inside, one belonging to the real estate agent and a mystery car that could have been anyone. She assumed it had to be someone interested in buying the property and judging the size of the vehicle, she figured it was an entire family.

Her stomach dropped.

Ebony parked her truck discreetly on the other side of the forest in a small opening hidden by trees. She lightly jogged over to her camp and let out a sigh of relief, seeing her tent and belongings undisturbed. She took out her infrared binoculars and scanned the tree line. The usual catlike shapes moved around the forest, but Ebony audibly gasped when she saw a human-shaped heat signature on the edge.

She grabbed a Glock and sprinted towards the shape, wondering who was dumb enough to go out there. Could it be the real estate agent? No, he seemed focused on selling, not having the time or gumption to wander away from money.

Could it be one of the parents? No, that didn't seem right either. Perhaps, it was the daughter. Had to be. Only thing made sense considering her brain wasn't fully developed and the lack of maturity.

"Fucking, kids," she mumbled to herself, grabbing her gear and rushing into the woods.

12

T HE MILKMAN NEVER SAW them coming.

A thick fog rolled in from the Wisconsin forest bordering the curving road. The dark shades of brown and green became soft and hazy. Drizzle pitter-pattered on the truck's windshield, slowly fogging up the laminated glass. The milkman pressed the defrost button. Heat felt good on his skin, warming his bones, but the air made the drive somewhat uncomfortable. He lifted his semi-pleated cap, scratched his black hair, digging into his scalp, and wiped the sweat from his furrowed brow. The sound of rain coming down was soothing, and his eyelids grew heavy. He grabbed a capped container of chocolate milk from his chilled lunchbox, and downed half of the refreshing liquid, hoping it would give him more life.

He turned up the volume, listening to his favorite podcast Agitated Arcane. Helped him stay up to date on the hottest UFO news, UAP developments, conspiracy theories, and esoteric knowledge to date.

"Last week, UAPs were seen flying over the Gulf of Iran. So get this, the U.S. Navy, an entire fleet of our biggest and baddest, shot down a flying sphere while another UAP disappeared into a glowing flash of light."

"Astounding stuff."

"Can't even make this up if I tried, Mick. The Government is releasing documents and whistleblowers are coming to the forefront, but one of my sources recently revealed that—"

The satellite radio station glitched and white static roared in the milkman's ears. The milkman messed with the knobs, struggling to turn down the noise. Something darted across the road, a moist flash of red fur resembling the outline of a mountain lion, but leaner. He rubbed his eyes, thinking he saw a naked woman on all fours, just hairier.

Get it together. Must be slipping into dream territory. Wake up!

The milkman lightly smacked his face and rolled his neck before clenching the steering wheel. He replayed the image through his mind, disgusted and slightly aroused at the same time. Something about the beast was attractive and he didn't know how to make sense of it. Best to bring this up to his therapist friend Charlie when he returned home. Buddy could make sense of the symbolism, stemming from his overactive subconscious.

The milkman turned down the volume, needing quiet, ears still ringing. He took a deep belly breath to steady his nerves. A soft face with dimples, short black hair, pearl earrings, and round eyes rose to the surface of his mind, helping his nerves reset. *Maybe I should give Vanessa a call, check in with her, and maybe flirt a bit...*

He missed her, missed the nights they cuddled on the couch watching cheesy Bollywood films, missed the karaoke sessions in the car, and the shared moments of connection. The simple rituals brought him comfort and balance. Picking up his cellphone, he scrolled through his recent calls, pausing on her name. His finger hovered over the contact with heart emojis next to it and—-

The left side of the truck was hit by something large and fast, rocking the vehicle off balance. Suspension groaning. Freaking out, the milkman jutted his right arm out, gripping the edge of the passenger seat and his left hand flattened against the ceiling for stability.

Fuckmefuckmefuckmefuckmefuckmefuckme.

Crazy thing about it, the milkman had never been in a car accident in his 28 years of existence and the road was empty and he'd been driving at a safe speed. Wet roads didn't scare him and this one was well-paved with no potholes, fallen trees or natural obstructions whatsoever. It made no sense why the wheels were screeching, made no sense why a small amount of piss trickled down his thigh, made no sense why the truck was skirting off the road and tumbling through the mud into the trees.

The milkman's head banged against something metal, and his limbs slammed against parts of the interior he didn't previously know existed. He never realized how soft and fragile the human body was until that very moment when everything seemed to hurt in new ways, and he wasn't sure what was broken, sprained or bruised.

Blood dripped down his nostrils as he struggled to release his seat belt sitting upside down, and take inventory of the damage done to his body. The polyester webbing finally snapped back, freeing him from his seat. He crawled out the broken window, ignoring the pieces of shattered glass jabbing his skin, embedding themselves into his flesh and the weird sounds outside.

Part of him was detached from reality, hanging onto a loose rope of pain, suffering, and confusion. The trees shook in weird patterns, swaying unevenly, making him question the veracity of his perception and question his mental faculties.

Groaning, he slowly stood, inspecting the wreckage rather than facing the scarlet map of bruises and wounds punctuating every muscle group. The milk truck sat upside down in the wet mud, wheels still spinning, and a massive dent was on the left side.

The milkman was unsure how to handle a situation like this. Nothing in orientation or his monthly training covered this scenario. He was tired and bleeding and he just wanted to go to sleep. His head hurt as if a significant amount of the inner insulation had been torn out and his thoughts weren't flowing the way he was accustomed to. In times of distress, he leaned on his logic, but his mind was foggy and slow-moving. Had to be the injuries he figured.

Am I in shock? Is this how those people on those survival shows feel? Get your head right. Solutions. Think of solutions. The phone. Grab your phone and call the local authorities. They'll help get this sorted out. And you can finally get some damn sleep.

A branch snapped in the distance, and the milkman swore he heard a cat's meow drift from behind the truck. He wished he had brought a weapon with him, but he didn't feel the need. No one robbed the milkman or a milk truck of all things.

Feeling somewhat silly, the milkman decided he'd investigate the sound to gain some emotional security. Maybe give the lone cat a bit of attention.

Get over yourself, it's just a stray cat. Probably lapping up some spilled milk.

Vanessa owned a cute Siamese cat that he fed on occasion. He couldn't wait to see her again and tell her about this absurd story over dinner and drinks so they could laugh about his ungrounded paranoia.

The visualization boosted his mood temporarily, softening the tension entwined in his body. The meows multiplied the closer he came to the back of the truck, and the tension returned, paralyzing his body as if there was an imaginary line he couldn't cross. Trees creaked and birds twittered in the darkness. Something inside him told him to turn around, some ancestral part of his DNA that recognized danger churned his stomach. Still, he ignored the physical siren flashing red in his mind, his ego needing to prove the feeling wrong by any means.

Nothing could have prepared him for the sight, let alone the overwhelming smell of fresh milk. It was sweet, but nauseating. Six cat women, that was the best word he could come up with to describe them, lapped at a pool of milk spilling from the jugs in the back of the truck. Their eyes shone in the darkness like yellow marbles underneath the moonlight. Soft muscular bodies covered in red fur moved through the mud on all fours, eyes fixated on the milkman.

He froze, not sure if he should run or find his way back to the road. The milkman was no wildlife expert, but he knew this wasn't normal and that he'd stumbled onto the fantastic, something that was far from the norm in his mundane life. He imagined the co-hosts of Agitated Arcane enjoying this Fortean encounter and possibly inviting him on future episodes. The possibility gave him comfort.

Part of him was in a state of awe while another felt a primal fear take over his body. He understood why people weren't able to take good photos in the midst of the miraculous. His particular situation was much more dire, and he became hyper aware of the sweat swelling in his armpits as well as his groin.

One cat woman stood, breasts heaving, and slowly strode towards him. Her flesh and fur glistened beautifully in the slats of moonlight.

Hissing.

The warning cry broke his reverie, and he ran towards the road, milk sloshing inside his stomach. The milkman pumped his legs and glanced behind him, seeing three cat women stalking him. Snot ran down his upper lip, covered in dried blood, and the cold air made his lungs burn from exertion.

Breathing in a ragged fashion, he wished he had listened to his buddy Rick, who nagged him about the importance of owning a firearm.

You never know bro, you never know. Motherfuckers are unhinged these days. You need protection no matter how big you are.

He could hear his friend's words rolling through his pounding head and wondered if he'd see the day he could tell his friend how right he was. The milkman always thought Rick was just a gun nut, potentially missing a few screws, but now he realized the importance of protection.

Lesson learned?

The cats moved faster as he struggled to ascend the muddy hill, sneakers sinking into the tread marks left behind by the truck's wheels. One of the cats shoulder-checked him and he went flying into the grass. A fiery lance of pain shot through his body as he saw her come closer, milk dripping down her furred face.

Whiskers twitching.

"Get away from me," the milkman weakly yelled, scooting backward.

The milkman threw a right hook, catching the cat in the cheek. He felt a satisfying crack as he connected. That satisfaction didn't last long because she snorted and shook the blow off.

Drizzle had transitioned into a cold rain, and the milkman shivered, not dressed well enough for the weather conditions. He got up and ran faster, hands and feet finally gaining purchase in the mud. Heaving himself upward, he was pulled right back down by several powerful paws, curled around his calves, into the dirt. The smell of raw earth tinged with milk made him sick to his stomach.

Hot breath kissed his neck, and sharp teeth flashed in the darkness, paws pinning him down. His lips were bitten off his face along with a portion of his cheek, the bottom one dangled like a worm barely hanging by a shred of skin. The muscular folds dangled from the cat creature's mouth before she devoured it like a snack.

The milkman's face bled profusely, and he had a hard time breathing. Water rained into the gaping wound, and he wondered if plastic surgery could fix it. *Maybe it's not as bad as it feels*, but he knew that was wishful thinking.

The trees shifted, branches groaning with the weight of more cat creatures. Their eyes gleamed like distant stars, and the voyeuristic nature of their stares, made him wish this entire thing would end. He was tired of feeling sharp pain, mud seeping through his clothes, and the threat of the cat creatures looming overhead.

He winced as the cat creature ran its thick tongue over the wound, licking the blood. Another one licked a scratch on his cheek, purring softly, and he felt like this was a sick form of grooming. The milkman kneed the cat creature that consumed his lips and it yelped in pain. The other cat creatures were so startled by the attack they released his arms and legs. He took advantage of the moment, and stumbled to his feet, skirting around the truck and taking off, stumbling much deeper into the woods.

When he looked behind him, he was surprised to see they were no longer chasing him. His face stung and he cursed himself for not grabbing his phone earlier. He sat by a rotting log, making himself still, hoping he'd be able to survive the night if he made himself small and quiet.

The sound of a cat meowing close by made him hold his breath. The meow turned into a soft purr. This calmed the milkman, knowing the cat had to be feeling good and not searching for prey. *But why did they let me escape? It made no sense.*

He knew house cats weren't carnivores, but these weren't ordinary housecats. These were huge, human-sized cats with big brains and even bigger claws.

The purrs heightened in volume and transitioned into a screeching howl that made the milkman's stomach tighten. He gripped the log behind him, wishing he could melt into the decaying piece of wood and tune out the frightening sounds.

13

"REMAIN CALM," JAYLEN TRIED assuring the family, but he wasn't quite sure if he believed his own words. Anxiety and paranoia had him in a vicious chokehold, and he knew this sale was most likely fucked. Something about this unexpected turn of events chipped his confidence and upbeat demeanor. "Everything's going to be alright."

"No, everything won't be *all right*," Tobias said, racking his shotgun, an intense seriousness dripping off his large frame.

"Oh god, Oliver, our baby Lily is all alone in the woods," Clara said, hanging onto Oliver's arm like the only solid thing that was keeping her from being swept away by her own turbulent emotions.

"This isn't the time for hysterics, Clara," Oliver said in a firm tone. "Like Jaylen said, we have to remain calm."

"Should you tell them?" Barbara said, hands trembling. "Maybe you should. I mean, it is their daughter."

"Tell them what?" Jaylen asked, curious, but wanting to quiet his racing thoughts.

How could this get any worse?

"Yeah, tell us what?" Oliver said, hands on his hips. Jaylen could tell the man was trying to stay strong, put on a mask of strength and stability, but the cracks in his demeanor were too large to hide.

Barbara and Tobias whispered among one another, too low for the group to understand.

"We have a fucking right to know," Clara screeched. "Tell us, please!"

"Jaylen, may I have a word in private?" Tobias asked.

"Of course."

Jaylen and Tobias walked off to the side until they were out of earshot.

"So what's up?" Jaylen said.

"Their daughter is in grave danger."

Jaylen's stomach dropped. "From what? Bears? I'm not quite following you."

"Something much worse."

"What can be worse than a goddamn bear?"

"I'm afraid to say, they have an ancient name, but they're a form of cat creature that resembles humans."

"You're fucking with me." Jaylen said. "Cat creatures? Come the fuck on."

"Do you see me laughing?"

Jaylen inspected the old man's face, wrinkles pinched in an expression that screamed life or death.

He was telling the truth or at least what he believed to be the truth.

"I assure you my mind is healthy. What I'm saying may sound far-fetched, but if you go into those woods, you'll see things that'll make you regain faith in God."

Those words made Jaylen's skin crawl, and he imagined these cat creatures somewhere in the darkness, tearing the poor girl apart. Still, he questioned the truthfulness of the old man's statement. Maybe his mind had become warped from being isolated on this property for far too long.

What if these cat creatures were simply mountain lions or bobcats? That would make a lot more sense than cat creatures.

"You don't believe me," Tobias said.

"I'm sorry, Tobias, I'm stressed the fuck out and I'm struggling to imagine these cat creatures. Feels like something out of a horror movie."

"Come with me," Tobias said, nodding his head towards the woods. "That's the only way."

Jaylen wondered if this man was off his rocker, being sincere or a mixture of both. He started into the old man's eyes once again, analyzing him. He seemed healthy for his age, and nothing prior to this seemed off, but still...

The sincerity won him over, but he had a looming concern.

"I'll come with you," Jaylen said, bracing himself for the expedition, never expecting himself to be part of a search party on a farm in Wisconsin, of all places. If he could bring their daughter back, maybe Oliver would feel like he had to follow though with purchasing the land. "But I need a weapon. I can't be in these woods empty-handed."

Jaylen owned a few firearms, but these were safely stored away in gun cases back in New York. Every state had different laws and hula hoops you had to jump through to travel with a gun. The headache wasn't worth it, but he questioned that logic, wishing he had looked up Wisconsin laws at the very least.

Tobias opened his mouth, but before he could speak, Barbara stepped in, offering up a Glock.

"I have you covered."

Jaylen took the gun and inspected it, noting the good condition of the firearm. He felt a lot more relaxed with this Glock in his hands, and a portion of tension dissolved from his chest.

"You know how to shoot that?" Tobias asked.

"Yeah, I own a Glock 19."

"Great."

Jaylen noticed the large man's disposition soften, learning he knew how to operate a gun.

"Is this really necessary?" Oliver said, crossing his arms. "These guns?"

"Yes," Tobias said. "Come on before the sun sets."

"I'm not going," Oliver said, gazing at Tobias and Jaylen. He stuck his index finger out, which trembled slightly. "This is your fucking fault and your fault."

"I think you should go," Clara said softly. "It's our daughter..."

"What part of I'm not going do none of you understand?" Oliver said, hands gesturing wildly. "Our daughter's underdeveloped brain led her to believe that it was a good idea to wander off into these woods."

"So it's our daughter's fault?"

"Yes and no," Oliver said, frustrated. He looked towards the trees, fear present in his voice. "It's a nuanced situation where multiple people are at fault."

"I thought you were better than this," Clara's voice cracked. "I barely recognize you as the man I married."

"You two go take care of this," Oliver commanded, steadying his tone. "I'll deal with her."

Tobias kissed Barbara on the lips passionately before giving her a tight hug.

"Be careful," she said.

"I'll be fine and look out for these two," Tobias said.

"I will," she said. "I love you."

"I love you too."

Jaylen didn't like the depth and intensity woven into this display of love. It made him feel like he wasn't stepping into some ordinary woods, but something much more dangerous than he anticipated. He wondered if he should call his wife and kids; maybe leave a heartfelt voice note, but he decided to wait. He had to see what was going on for himself. Just for good measure, he checked his phone battery and signal; both seemed to be good to go. If he had to contact anyone, he was confident he'd be able to do it even in the heart of the woods.

Tobias' countenance hardened and his grip tightened on his shotgun, and he walked towards the tree line. Jaylen followed suit and easily caught up to the large man. They gave one another a nod before disappearing into the greenery.

14

F UMING WITH RAGE AND control issues, Oliver watched the old man and the real estate agent disappear into the woods. They tried to convince him to join the search party as he eyed the dark tree line, briefly contemplating stepping into the foliage, fear slithered through his chest and he reminded himself that this was beneath him.

This was their fault. Not his. Why should I have to ruin a good shirt? They're able-bodied men who should easily fix this inconvenience.

The real estate agent invited him and his family to this dilapidated farm, the only selling point being the hunting grounds. The old man didn't warn them about the terrors of the woods and the animals lurking inside. He was prepared to call his lawyer if anything happened to his sweet pumpkin Lily.

What a fucking nightmare.

He remembered when Clara shot him a look of utter disgust his way when he refused to go into the woods. That was not his responsibility, but his wife thought outdated gender standards applied to him. That he should put his life on the line, when he was the provider for his family.

How ludicrous. Clara's sweet, but she's dense. Doesn't see the bigger picture. We all have a role to play.

Still, it was hard to shake the memory of her searing gaze and the way she walked away from him. Her usually warm demeanor had become downright cold. The frigid shift in energy disturbed him. Thinking about it only fanned the flames of anger inside his gut. He stormed over to an atrocious-looking scarecrow. He punched it in the gut, tufts of hay spilling out. Something about its stomach felt too soft, too much give for something constructed from hay and sticks of wood.

It looked down at him as it took a beating. Oliver threw a mean right hook that broke its button nose in two. The eyes seemed to be seared into its oblong head. The expression was solemn as if the scarecrow was patiently waiting for Oliver to run out of energy, and hop down off the wooden pole and give the man a beating of his own.

Oliver pushed aside his silly train of thought and continued to throw sloppy blows, never having had any formal training in combat sports, channeling all of the hot anger into his fists, yelling at its blank face. He yelped as he jammed his finger, trying to shake the pain out of his hand.

Fucking scarecrow. I should sue the pants off the owners.

With his good hand, he ripped out tufts of hay, wanting to destroy its world, disfigure its anatomy. Something thick and red slid against a hole he created.

Fuck is this?

He pulled out tufts of hay until it moved forward, palming the lodged object. It was slimy and red. Oliver wanted to wipe the residue off on his pants, but he wasn't entirely sure what it consisted of and the possibility of him ruining his pants was high up on his list of things he didn't want.

The thing slipped out followed by a single black braid of hair covered in eggshells. He picked up the red object that might have been a heart. It was bruised and had strange symbols carved into the flesh. He wasn't sure what to make of it, but it made him uneasy.

Oliver looked around, not sure where his wife or the old woman had gone. The men were most likely in the woods and a sense of profound isolation struck him. Looking up at the ruined scarecrow only worsened his feeling of unease and paranoia began to drip in. He wanted to shake this foolishness out of his mind, but something told him that he'd done something wrong, something beyond his understanding and privileged lifestyle.

The other scarecrow he spotted on the property seemed to be ruined as well. He knew they protected the farm from birds who wanted to eat their crops, but something about these gave him the sense that they had a purpose beyond protecting the fields from birds.

He wished he could ask the owners questions about these scarecrows, feeling like that would put him at ease. He wondered how Lily was feeling all alone in the woods and felt concerned about her safety and well-being.

Tobias was gone, but Barbara was still on the property. Perhaps he could find her and ask some questions rather than take out his rage on some scarecrows. In some respects, his body felt less weighted by the anger he had accumulated that afternoon, but in other ways, his negative emotions only heightened after the act.

As he took quick strides away from the scarecrow in search of Barbara and his wife, a nugget of fear took root and grew bigger with each passing moment. He had no idea what type of horrible fruit this fear would give birth to, but he wasn't looking forward to it.

15

"YOU THINK SHE'S STILL alive?" Jaylen asked, trailing Tobias as they entered the woods. Branches scraped against his suit jacket and pants, scratching the expensive fabric. He tried his best to ignore the ruined suit and the money going down the drain.

"I hope so," Tobias said.

"You didn't answer my question," Jaylen said, slightly frustrated by the man's lack of a straight answer. "If you had to bet money, what would you say?"

"I'm not a gambling man."

"C'mon give me something, Tobias. Are we wasting our time out here or what?"

Tobias grew frustrated at the man's incessant questions, but suppressed his anger. He reminded himself that Jaylen hadn't seen the cat creatures and this possibility was hard for any man to imagine. Not too long ago, he doubted what he saw even after killing one outside the barn. He thought maybe he'd lost his mind or had a walking dream.

The fact that Jaylen decided to venture into the woods, said a lot about the man's character. He was wary of Jaylen at first, but his respect for him ballooned considerably in the last hour. He could push aside the annoyance. The man deserved that much.

"Going after an innocent girl and saving her from harm is not wasting our time," Tobias said. "We're taking action and that's all that matters."

"So, you think she's still alive."

"I said I hope so."

"You know what?" Jaylen threw his hands in the air. "You win, I'm letting it go."

Tobias continued trudging forward, looking for signs of the daughter's passage. He bent down, knees creaking, as he brushed aside some leaves and inspected the dirt for shoe prints. Instead, he found something so much worse.

"Look at this..." Tobias said, gesturing for Jaylen to see what he uncovered in the wet earth. He knew they'd pick up the trail sooner than later.

Jaylen bent down, noticing the plethora of paw prints, his finger lightly tracing the indentation in the ground. Tobias watched as the glow of recognition and understanding spread across Jaylen's face. A mixture of concern and deep thought flickered through his eyes, and he opened his mouth to speak.

"These are huge..." Jaylen said, deep in thought. "Maybe they're cougars or mountain lions?"

"Cougars are mountain lions, so yes some are in Wisconsin, but usually in the Northern parts," Tobias said. "I've lived here for decades and I assure you, these are no mountain lions."

"I'm sorry, but it's hard for me to imagine these cat monsters you're talking about," Jaylen said. "I've never seen anything like that."

"I know it sounds like hogwash, but you'll see," Tobias said. "And once you do, it's hard to unsee. We think we've analyzed and researched every inch of this Earth, but there are aspects that go beyond the normal threshold of perception. Fortean aspects that are extraordinary and frightening to even think about."

"I get what you're saying. Kinda like angels and God. Things we can't see, but know are there."

"Yeah, but these things aren't divine. Can't say they're evil either. They're something *else*."

They moved deeper into the forest, walking in silence. The sounds of leaves crunched beneath their feet, birds chirped and trilled, and a bubbling brook flowed nearby. If Tobias was in any other part of Wisconsin, the forest ambiance would have put him at ease and made him feel relaxed. However, it had the opposite effect on him, making him grow tense and anxious. The air was cool, but sweat ran down the small of his back.

He wouldn't dare voice his fears out loud on account of not wanting to scare Jaylen shitless, but he was scared. Scared that the girl had been torn limb by limb or her entrails had been clawed out of her stomach. A montage of grisly scenes played inside his mind's theater, too extreme and detailed for the movie screen.

Tobias kept expecting to hear a growl or one of their distinctive meows. Sounds that made him want to high-tail it in the opposite direction, but he kept moving forward. He couldn't blame Oliver for not joining the search party, but he had no idea what horrors existed in this forest, what these creatures were capable of. Still, he couldn't see himself abandoning his daughter and hoping for the best. They were complete strangers to Oliver. Why would you put your own daughter's safety and welfare in a stranger's hands?

He wasn't a father and didn't know the full responsibility that came with the role, but he had paternal instincts. A natural inclination and care for those who were innocent, weaker, etc. That same inclination drove him to venture into the woods despite his body's protests and desire for self-preservation.

A scream pierced through the woods and Tobias paused, trying his best to pinpoint the girl's location. Jaylen's face grew pale, hearing the scream and his grip tightened around the Glock in his hands. Tobia knew she wasn't far, being accustomed to the forest.

"Let's go," Tobias said, signaling for Jaylen to follow him.

Tobias ran as fast as his old legs could manage, not caring about the pain shooting through chest, his body protesting the physical activity. They ran east, branches and foliage whipping past their faces, and the mournful song of a bird calling.

He silently prayed they weren't too late.

16

E BONY BENT DOWN AND tightened the laces on her Russell Moccasin Co. Wyman 90 hunting boots. She owned this pair for seven years, and they had become her go-to when it came to cryptid hunting. The Walnut Timberjack leather was comfortable, water-resistant, highly durable, and above all else, whisper quiet. She stalked several cryptids in various terrains and was surprised by the lack of noise her boots produced. She didn't care about purses, but she appreciated the rich brown patina the boots developed over time.

She moved into the woods, feeling a distinct shift in the atmosphere. The sounds of the typical wildlife were present, but they seemed on edge. Even the bird songs seemed tense, suffocated, and off-key. The cryptid's unsettling presence was felt by all that inhabited these woods.

The leaves didn't even crunch underneath her boots. She gripped her Glock 20 with a 30-round extended magazine, knowing the semi-auto would give her the inner security she needed. Her nose twitched, and she sniffed the air.

Is that milk? This makes no sense whatsoever.

Ebony followed the scent of spoiled milk, the trail getting stronger and stronger. It made her want to vomit, but she had an iron-clad stomach. She continued forward, tightening her grip on the gun in her hand.

Fifteen feet ahead, she noticed a truck upside down with multiple dents in the side, tires in the air, coated in green foliage. A cartoonish cow was painted on the side of the truck that seemed familiar.

How did this happen? She thought, wondering if this was an accident or if the driver had been run off the road by the cat creatures.

She moved around the truck and was shocked to see two cat women drinking milk from small glass containers. Red fur covered their athletic frames, hints of their muscle could be seen in their legs. They didn't notice Ebony's presence, too caught up in indulging their thirst. Their furry stomachs were bloated and extended outward.

One sniffed the air and snapped her head towards Ebony. Ebony didn't hesitate to raise her Glock and let off a shot that ripped through the cat woman's head, brain matter and skull fragments painted the tree behind her a crimson red.

The other one was on all fours, running towards Ebony, anger dripping from her frame. Ebony pulled the trigger and the cat woman somehow dodged the shot and it whizzed past its ear. The bitch moved faster than she had expected and it leapt into the air, claws out.

Ebony let off two shots: one tore through its neck while the other hit the center of mass. The force of the shots threw the creature off balance and it fell into thick grass at Ebony's feet.

Two down.

She wondered how many more were roaming the woods, thinking back to the infrared bodies she'd spotted earlier. The numbers were too high to count. Part of her wished she could take the body, fly back to France, and collect her payday, but she wouldn't be able to sleep at night knowing a teenage girl was still out there. The blood on her hands would be too much to bear, and she had the power to return her safely to her parents. She just hoped the girl managed to stay alive up until now.

It wouldn't be long until the other cat women made their way to this part of the woods. Ebony moved into the shadows and carefully crept through the brush, waiting to see how many would make their appearance known.

After about seven minutes of waiting, five of them sprinted into the clearing. They slowed down and stood on their haunches, walking upright towards the dead bodies. A few licked the bodies, and the cat women let out a mournful sigh as they realized they were dead.

Ebony weighed her options. *Should I kill them off now or wait until they disperse? Maybe they'll lead me straight to the girl.*

She figured that was the best course of action, and she waited as they picked up the limp bodies and tossed them over their shoulders.

Ebony followed them, making sure not to get too close. She moved deeper into the forest and noticed the space darkening, and the branches became sharper.

What she saw chilled her to her core and made her think twice about taking on this job.

17

J AYLEN FELT AS IF he and Tobias had been running for miles. The uneven terrain made his ankles hurt, and he wished he had opted for more comfortable dress shoes instead of the boxy coffee brown Ferragamos that housed his tired feet. He wasn't sure why he had to show out, put on an air of luxury and wealth. It wasn't far from the truth, but he found himself still wanting to impress others.

He looked down at Tobias' work boots caked with mud, grime, and dried fluids. The boots looked well beyond broken in, but these weren't made for running either. The old man's feet had to be aching. Still, the old man was one hundred percent comfortable with himself and didn't give a fuck what people thought. He wondered how long this transformation took and if he would ever reach it.

"Slow down," Tobias said, coming to a standstill, taking in sharp, labored breaths, and leaned against a tree. His face was red and ruddy, and Jaylen could tell the old man hadn't exerted this much energy in ages.

He was surprised Tobias kept up the pace as long as he did.

"You think we're close?" Jaylen asked. He felt antsy, ancestral memory kicking into fifth gear. They were nearing *something*; he could feel it. His wife would probably call this intuition.

"Hold on," Tobias said, gasping for air. His features contorted into a canvas of pain and overexertion. Skin gray and ashy.

"You okay?" Jaylen asked. "You're not looking so hot."

Tobias clutched the left side of his chest and vomited something black into a bush. He wiped his mouth with the back of his hand, groaning in pain. His other palm skidded across the tree bark, blood smearing down the oak ridges.

"Tobias! Jaylen rushed over, hooking his arms underneath the old man's armpits, struggling to keep him up. The weight was too much, and they both tumbled to the ground.

Jaylen rolled over, brushing dead leaves out of his hair, and Tobias wasn't moving. His eyes were closed, and he seemed deathly still. Jaylen lightly smacked Tobias' reddened cheeks, but he was unresponsive. He brought his right hand to the side of Tobias' neck, index finger lightly pressed against the skin, checking his pulse, but there were no signs of life. The old man's brown eyes stared at the concrete grey sky.

Heart attack.

Jaylen recognized it, remembering his cousin, who everyone referred to as Uncle Duck, having a heart attack back when he was only 9. He'd been eating dinner and nursing a warm beer, cracking jokes, a smile smeared across his face. That smile mutated into something painful, his lips curling in a strange fashion, his hand gripping his chest, and he collapsed to the ground. His family freaked out, calling an ambulance that arrived far too late to save him.

"Tobias, wake up!"

The logical part of Jaylen's brain knew it was fruitless, trying to make the old man wake up, but couldn't accept what happened. This was Murphy's Law in action–if anything could go wrong, it would.

Fuck Murphy. Fuck these woods. Still, the girl...you can't leave her alone. You have to find her and close this sale.

Jaylen closed the old man's eyelids and muttered a soft prayer for him. He shook his head, realizing he was alone and directionless in the woods. Mentally steeling himself, he watched the shadows darken around him. The sun was going down and light was limited. He looked around for his phone, found the device, and noticed the signal was gone.

He wanted to take out his anger on the phone, imagining himself chucking the thing as far as he could. Instead, he took a breath, imagining his wife's soft voice reassuring him that everything was going to be alright, moving him far away from making dumb emotional decisions.

I don't know if it will.

Jaylen suppressed the intense urge to turn around and shoved the phone into his pocket. He didn't have many vices outside of making money and the pursuit of luxurious items, but he wished he could do something immediate like lighting a cigarette or downing a flask of tequila. He didn't care for the taste or smell of cigarettes and he only enjoyed drinking champagne with his wife Nala.

Scooping up the old man's shotgun put his slight shaking at ease. If anyone else was around, he'd laugh it off and blame it on the rapidly dropping temperature, but the truth was far from being underdressed—-he was frightened and couldn't remember the last time he experienced this emotion so intensely. As he pulled the strap around his shoulder, he wondered how he would break the news to Barbara. The thought alone made his head throb with a dull pressure, and his palms sweat.

He moved deeper into the woods, rehearsing the potential words, but all he heard was his obituary being read aloud by a deep voice that he couldn't shake.

18

THE MILKMAN REMEMBERED GETTING interviewed for the job. He thought it would be something easy, something temporary to hold him over until he got back on his feet. A layover, he jokingly referred to it. His next destination would be ten times better.

He smoothed out his button-up shirt and his black tie. Dressing up showed effort; it displayed a certain level of care and consideration. A thoughtful appearance reflected a number of attributes that might carry over into the workplace.

A woman named Kylie, who wore a suit jacket several sizes too large for her small frame, asked him a list of questions on a coffee-stained piece of paper while she puffed her vape pen in the cramped office. A small fan moved from side to side, circulating the hot air in the room, and ruffling her brown curly hair. She asked a series of questions off a piece of paper he felt she'd taken from an AI chatbot. They were easy enough until one stunned the milkman, causing him to pause and reflect before spitting out his next answer.

"What is your relationship with milk?" she asked.

He smoothed out his tie as he thought about the question and the underlying purpose behind it. She sucked on her vape, waiting for the answer, seeming as if she was being swallowed by enormous folds in the wrinkles of her suit jacket.

Was this a clever way to gain insight into my morals, discover my stance on animal cruelty or maybe she was a health nut that measured men's masculinity and workplace value by how much raw milk they consumed?

He didn't fucking know the angle or the intentions, so he went out on a limb and freestyled his answer.

"Milk is good. I like raw milk, oat milk, chocolate milk, and almond milk on occasion. I drink it with my cereal and I dip my cookies in a cold glass. I believe it's good for bones and that's my final answer."

The interviewer blew out a puff of smoke that obscured her round face and smelled like blueberries.

"Wonderful," she coughed into her small fist. "You're hired."

The job was easy enough. He woke every morning at 5 am, made it to the milk processing plant by 6:20 am and promptly started his shift at 6:30 am. The truck was already packed by a small team of men and he was given his route. He'd drive around different roads every day, delivering glass jugs of milk to random doorsteps.

People were surprisingly kind, some going so far as to give him a nice tip or kind words. The monetary rewards combined with the words of affirmation made him feel like he was doing something worthwhile, something that impacted society in a positive way.

Men needed purpose, otherwise they're lost, bitter creatures reeling into darkness. The milkman had no plans of returning to that place, that state of mind, but ever since that freak accident with the delivery truck, he questioned his purpose, his place in the whole scheme of things, and realized it meant nothing in the wilderness.

The milkman thought he'd escaped the cat creatures, but it was only a dream. He'd been awakened by something wet assaulting his face, stinging his eyes and open wounds. Struggling to get to his feet, he snorted and coughed out the foul liquid.

Hot piss stained his uniform which was already smeared with mud, dead plants, and other detritus. He looked and felt like a bag of ass.

A cat creature pissed on him while he slept. It scraped the ground, over and over with its claws. The milkman didn't understand this behavior, but he was thankful his own bladder was empty and his mouth was dry, otherwise, he would have pissed himself out of sheer fright. Six more of them lay in the clearing, licking their paws while one tore into a partially eaten deer carcass. The cat's pink snout was painted in thick coats of blood as it devoured the innards.

The milkman slowly sat back down in a dry spot as the cat creatures eyed him. He had no idea how to read cats let alone animals in general. He was never much of a pet person, not wanting to take on that extra level of responsibility and his parents could barely take care of themselves, let alone him growing up. Plus, he was on the road most of the time delivering milk so pets weren't a realistic option for him.

Either way, the collective watchful eye of the cat creatures put him on edge, and anxiety thrummed through his chest and arms. And that foul smell of piss embedded into the fabric stuck to his body made his nostrils twitch and his stomach turn. He couldn't remember the last time he felt so helpless.

A gunshot went off, and the milkman instinctively ducked, hands covering his head. Five of the cat creatures ran towards the sound, leaving him alone with the remaining two.

This is your chance. Run for it. You might not get another shot.

The milkman took deep breaths, hyping himself up. *Now or never.*

He took a tentative step, *snapping* a twig with the weight of his foot. The other cat creatures roused from their sleep, stretching their limbs in a sensual way.

They moved closer, and he sat back down, praying they would leave him the fuck alone.

The cat creatures groomed one another, and he cursed himself for not retrieving his phone from the wreckage.

He didn't have a large circle of friends, and his network of people was associates at most. His coworkers were somewhat strange and his job role required him to mostly work on his own. There probably wasn't much evidence of him fishtailing into the woods. His boss probably thought he had stolen the truck and driven somewhere far, never to be heard from again. If he survived this ordeal, he knew he'd be without a job. No way in hell, they'd believe him bringing up cat creatures running him off the road. He couldn't blame them; the concept sounded ludicrous and drug-fueled.

Holding his head in his hands, he wondered if whoever let off the gunshots was still alive or dead. Part of him knew it was foolish, but there were gun fanatics in the backwoods who had an obscene amount of guns and artillery. Perhaps one of them was having a field day with these cat creatures, but his hope began to dwindle with each passing moment.

One of the cat creatures sauntered over and began picking leaves and twigs out of the milkman's hair, licking the center. Then she moved down and licked behind his ear, purring the entire time. The pleasurable sensation combined with the sensual sound of her purrs, made his dick grow hard.

Part of the milkman felt like he should be scared, but the fear melted away and he relaxed. He stared into the cat woman's eyes which seemed to glow with an essence that sucked him in like honey. The red fur didn't seem as thick, soft curves calling out to him, as she reminded him of Vanessa.

He looked down at her large breasts that seemed to swell, beckoning him forward. Without a second thought, he palmed the right one with his hand and brought his mouth to the brown nipple on the left. He sucked on it, enjoying the warm flesh against his cheek. Milk trickled down his tongue and it tasted sweet.

Everything around him seemed to intensify: the grass became a more vivid green, the air became crisp and rejuvenating, the sun rays ignited with a brightness that seemed to caress his face.

He squeezed her breast, relishing the milk coating his tongue and she moaned. His dick throbbed and he came inside his pants.

A gunshot went off, the cat creature's body jerked, and fell to the ground.

19

B ARBARA HAD NO IDEA her day would consist of consoling a mother and being worried sick about the woman's missing daughter while wondering where in the world the husband had wandered off to. He should be in the woods with the other men, she thought.

She trusted that Tobias would have this handled by nightfall, but the sun's fiery bottom sank into the horizon and she worried that things had become complicated and her heart beat much faster than it was accustomed to doing.

Clara sniffled, blowing her red nose over and over, tears streaming down her face. Barbara tried not to notice the large amount of mucus that came out of the mother's nose. A tower of tissues eclipsed her bowed head. The woman had a hell of a day and was grieving. Grieving the potential death of her daughter and the death of her marriage.

The woman had gone on and on about her husband's cowardice and Barbara saw the respect she once held for him slowly dissolving. It was a terrible sight to see, and tugged on her heartstrings. She couldn't imagine being without Tobias, and the sheer thought almost threw her into hysterics.

Keep it together, Barb. Don't let this woman see you crack; it'll only make her spiral. No time for that...

Barbara downed the rest of her lemonade and rubbed Clara's back in small circles. She could only focus on the task at hand and trust that Tobias and Jaylen would make it back safely. It took every ounce of her mental strength to ignore the round clock perched above the kitchen sink, the small hand *clicking.*

"C-can you do me a favor?" Clara sniffled.

"Anything. Just you name it."

"Can you check on my sorry excuse of a husband?" Clara asked. "Like what the fuck is he doing outside?"

"I'll go check on him," Barbara said. "Make yourself at home. We have plenty of tissues for you."

Clara pulled out another tissue and blew her nose. The mountain of tissues slouched to the side, teetering.

Barbara walked outside and went out into the cornfield, searching for Oliver. It didn't take long to find him pacing back and forth in front of a ruined scarecrow. Tufts of hay clenched in his hands. A terrible feeling stitched throughout her stomach, making her remember the other damaged scarecrows.

She had reassured Tobias that the lone sentry would be enough to hold the cat women at bay, knowing how much he hated working with the occult elements. That he could get around to fixing the others when he had time.

"Oliver, how are you?" she asked, concerned about the man, but even more concerned about what he had done to the scarecrow. That was their last line of defense.

"Not good," Oliver said, still pacing back and forth.

"Your wife was asking about you," she said. "Come inside."

His face soured hearing this. "Dumb cunt thinks she can judge me. Why isn't she out here? Probably having another meltdown in your living room."

Barbara didn't know how to respond, taking note of the way he was scraping the inside of his palm with his fingernail. She watched the area grow redder while heated words were being mumbled under his breath. She took a step back, feeling like the man was on the edge of an explosion, a breakdown or both. His incendiary energy made her feel uneasy.

"Your silence tells me everything I need to know," he said.

"W-we should head back inside," Barbara said. "Take a seat, unwind, and have a glass of lemonade."

"I don't want to head inside or drink your fucking lemonade."

Barbara gasped, and a blur of red fur sped by her peripheral. Her heart almost stopped and she had to remind herself to breathe, to get moving.

They're here. I knew they were coming, but I thought we had more time.

Oliver kept talking, yapping about his wife, completely unaware of the old woman's slow, but hurried retreat towards the entrance of her home. A cat creature leapt out of the stalks of corn and scratched his face, and another threw her full weight against his upper body, claws sinking into the soft tissue of his shoulder blades, tearing skin and fabric, exposing musculature.

Barbara watched three cat creatures swarm the man, and she tried her best to ignore his piercing screams. One came up with a stringy eyeball, playing with it like a ball of yarn. It flew in the air as a cat lay on her back, purring with glee.

The old woman jogged up the porch stairs, forcing herself to move much faster than she was accustomed to, breathing heavily, scared that the cat creatures might bound across the field any second to satiate their bloodlust. Thankfully, her fears weren't realized, and she made it inside without any trouble.

She quickly locked the door, hands still trembling.

"What's going on?" Clara said, nose red, carrying a handful of tissues.

"They're here."

"Who?" Clara asked, growing excited. "Your husband and the real estate agent found Lily. I knew they would."

"No, unfortunately, the men haven't made it back quite yet."

Clara's shoulders slumped. "Must be my cowardly husband coming to check on me."

"No, the cat creatures," Barbara said. "Stand back."

"Pardon, but did you just say cat creatures?"

Barbara twisted the second lock on the door and put down the heavy wooden bar that Tobias installed to reinforce the home's security. She moved from window to window, sweat forming in her armpits, closing the blinds. They didn't want to draw attention to themselves.

"Is Oliver okay?" Clara asked.

"Help me close the blinds," Barbara said.

"You didn't answer my question."

"You don't want to hear the answer."

Clara nodded and began to help close the remaining blinds. Her sniffling lessened and her disposition shifted towards a more fearful space.

Barbara searched for the other gun in the master bedroom, digging through the closet. They had plenty of ammo, but no need for an entire armory. Tobias protected her, but he probably had no idea how dire things had become during his absence.

She found the rifle hidden behind a pile of old dresses and hurried down the stairs.

"Are those cat women?" Clara asked, peeking through a set of blinds. "They look like cougars."

Barbara suppressed her irritation, gently grabbed Clara, ushered her away from the window, and guided her into the kitchen.

"Have a seat."

"Am I losing it, Barbara?" Clara's eyes were red-rimmed from crying. "I used to be on medication for my anxiety, but I haven't taken it in ages and now I'm hallucinating."

"No, you're not losing it. There are cat creatures out there and the only thing protecting us was the scarecrows until…"

"Until what?"

"Until your husband destroyed the last one. He seemed so worked up."

"I'm so confused," Clara cradled her head in her hands, hair hanging down in irregular strands of blonde. She seemed well put together when the family first arrived, but now her hair was in complete disarray. "Scarecrows, cat creatures…I knew moving to Wisconsin was a terrible idea. Should have never listened to Oliver."

"Well, honey, I'm not sure if this is the best time, but your husband is dead."

Barbara wasn't sure if it was too early, but her patience was running thin, and her grace was quickly evaporating. And it was only a matter of time until Clara found out the truth. Words held weight and consequences, but they were less severe when compared to seeing his body torn apart outside.

Clara shrugged.

"I'm going to give you something you need to hold onto, okay, and I need you to promise me that you won't freak out?"

"What?"

Barbara handed Clara a huge butcher knife, stained with blood from years of use on game and wildlife that Tobias personally killed.

"I-I can't."

"You can and you will," Barbara insisted, placing the handle in Clara's hand and closing her long fingers around it. "We need protection."

"I don't need *shit*," Barbara hissed.

"Talk to me like that again, and I'll throw your ass outside. Don't take my kindness for weakness, little girl."

Clara shrank in her chair. "I-I'm sorry."

"Apology accepted," Barbara said. "I need you to bring that fire back out and be prepared to use it on those monsters outside. They're coming and we're all we got for now."

Clara nodded solemnly as she tightened her grip on the handle and looked at her reflection in the blade. The grimness in her eyes scared her.

20

A MAN'S BODY WAS impaled on a large stick, one that most likely belonged to a scarecrow. The man's eyes were gouged out, deep lines ringing his orbital sockets. His face resembled a phantasm instead of something alive and breathing. His torso was covered in dried blood, and his groin was exposed, looking as if something had sliced it in half, the remains flopped in the wind.

Upon closer inspection, she noticed leaves and hay stuffed into the man's stomach, slick with blood. He seemed like he was in decent shape, perhaps a farmhand. She knew the cat creatures made short work of the man and posted him up as a warning for anyone who came too close to their camp. Ebony almost vomited at the sight. She'd seen her fair share of horrors during her term serving in the Navy Special Forces.

Moving through the Hindu Kush mountain range, less than a decade ago, her team was ambushed by a group of locals. The air was thin and hard to breathe, especially with the 50-pound ruck on her back, several layers of clothing under her desert digital camo uniform equipped with a M4A1 Carbine and a SOPMOD Kit. Sweat dripped down her hair, tied in a tight bun, soaking the bottom half of her tan beanie despite the brutally cold wind flowing through the towering peaks and sheer cliffs.

The wind played tricks on her mind, sounding like haunting voices bouncing off the deep valleys and rock faces. Over time, the voices became clearer, and she could almost hear them coalescing into something legible. Her mind couldn't put it together, but her right hand tightened around the pistol grip while her other clamped over the top rail, applying even more pressure. She thought the gun might break into pieces if the wind didn't cease.

They slowly trekked across a narrow, winding pass, and the point man suddenly collapsed. Blood trickled from a headshot and Ebony had to slow her breathing. She served with Holloway for three years and he was a reliable operator and a good friend. He did have an issue sitting still; he was a man who needed the military just as much as big Navy needed him. It was hard for her to see him as a civilian and transition into a nice, quiet life. That was a world he didn't belong in; this microcosm was all he was built for and now he was gone.

The squad moved in tandem, waiting for the attackers to make their presence known. A few minutes passed and then a dark shape swooped down from above. Ebony expected locals, but this thing had leathery flesh, several bloodshot eyes, and bat-like wings. Several green tip rounds ripped through the creature as it screeched in pain and dropped to the ground.

Several more creatures flooded the space, and she let muscle memory take over. Part of her wasn't sure if she was hallucinating or having a bad dream, but when one slashed her thigh, blood dripped down her leg and the cold slipped inside the wound, giving her a moment of respite. She held the buttstock firmly against her shoulder and mowed down the creatures. She watched her entire team get decimated as anger, confusion, and helplessness swirled around her chest.

The air smelled like ammonia, overripe fruit, and damp earth. She walked over the bodies of her brothers and the coriaceous creatures that were as large as men, but resembled bats, covered every inch of the ground. Muscles, bones, and tendons cracked and broke as she walked across the sea of bodies.

Ebony pulled out the large, bulky walkie-talkie off Holloway's hip, brought it to her mouth, gloved hands aching in the cold, and hissed into the SATCOM radio, "Blackout actual, this is Wraith, I repeat Blackout actual. Grid 42SLQ 8739 264. Requesting immediate CSAR. Over."

These cryptids were savages, but this decaying corpse was a symbol, a symbol designed to scare people away, a warning to all those who crossed this line that this was a point of no return. That you too, could get killed and turned into a human scarecrow if you weren't careful.

This was a clear sign of immense intelligence. She liked to gather as much information as she could on her targets before taking on a job, but sadly, cryptid documentation was highly classified or virtually non-existent, destroyed by fearful parties and occult groups. She had a few connections in high places that helped, but these were hit or miss.

This made things more thrilling for Ebony, but she preferred her cryptids on the dumb and dangerous side of the spectrum.

Ebony took heed, and everything in her considered saying fuck this job and go home. However, another part of her wanted to jump over this line and spit in the face of safety. Her mom always said she was a daredevil and a rebel at heart. Plus, Ebony loved a good challenge. She wanted to see if these cat creatures had what it took to tango with her and the diverse armory at her disposal. These furry fucks were dangerous, but so was Ebony, if not more.

Time for an inventory check.

First were the knives: a Smith & Wesson HRT fixed blade boot knife strapped to her right ankle housed in a nylon sheath, a Desert Fox drop point blade concealed in a Kydex sheath on her belt, one on the inside of her coat jacket, another on her forearm, and lastly, and a Mantis MK5B folding Karambit Flipper Black Hawkbill Blade hidden inside of her sports bra.

Second were the guns: a M4A1 carbine with an advanced combat optical gun sight, a suppressor, and white-light/IR illumination, her primary weapon of choice. The compact HK 45 would serve as her backup, firmly placed in her holster.

Third was the medicinal supplies: antiseptic wipes, aloe vera gel, antibiotic ointment, elastic bandages, iodine, hydrogen peroxide, bandages, gauze, and a SAM splint.

Ebony kept moving forward despite the human scarecrow and eventually saw a cat creature lounging in the grass while another one seemed to be entangled with a man. As she moved closer, he noticed him sucking on her tit and squeezing her other breast. The cat creature purred with pleasure.

What the fuck is going on?

Not one to ruminate on things too long, Ebony looked through her optical sight, lining up the cat's head in the crosshairs and pulled the trigger. Blood sprayed and it dropped to the ground. The other cat dashed to the left and pivoted to the right, attempting to evade Ebony's inevitable shot. She slowed her breathing, predicting its next movement, and pulled the trigger.

The bird calls went silent and Ebony heard the sounds of multiple bird wings flapping as they left the trees, looking for somewhere safer in the woods.

Ebony walked over, expecting a colony of cats to come out of the shadows or bound out of tree trunks, but nothing of the sort happened. The man was shaking as she approached him, eyes closed, and hands covering his head. He was missing his lips, white teeth and pink gums showing like a walking cadaver. Flesh had been ripped from his face, musculature exposed to the elements. Ebony knew it had to be painful.

"It's okay," Ebony said softly. "I'm not going to hurt you."

"I-I'm sorry, but it's not what you think," the milkman said, coming back to his senses.

"What? You sucking on her tits?"

"You saw that?" the milkman said, looking ashamed and embarrassed.

"All of it," Ebony said. "But don't worry, your business is your business."

"Oh okay, let's forget about that," the milkman said, nervously playing with his hair. "I wasn't sure if I'd ever see another human again."

He hugged Ebony, holding onto her as if she were the last human left in existence, not wanting to let go.

She cringed under the stranger's embrace. Part of her wanted to push him off, but she knew he'd probably seen things that would make people's skin crawl, and he'd probably need several years of intensive therapy to heal the trauma he experienced. He stepped back, and she noticed his uniform was torn up, ragged, and splotched with blood.

"Fuck."

"Fuck is right," he said. "You know about *them*, don't you?"

"Yeah," she said, not even hiding it.

"They're monsters," the milkman said. "Didn't know things like that existed."

"There are monsters worse than these things."

"I hope I never meet them," the milkman said, face wincing with every word spoken. "Thank you for saving me."

"I haven't saved you yet," Ebony said, looking around, knowing the cat creatures couldn't be too far off.

"What's your name?"

"Don't worry about it," she said. "I don't care to know yours either."

"What's up with the secrecy, huh?" the milkman said, looking suspicious. "Working for the government or some sort of secret branch? I've watched enough documentaries to know these types of things."

"Neither," Ebony said. "And don't believe everything you see online. There are disinformation agents planting seeds that lead you astray."

"Then who?"

Ebony shook her head. "Stop asking all of these invasive questions and follow me. And do your best not to be killed."

The milkman struggled to keep up as Ebony took long, quick strides through the woods.

"Where are we going?" the milkman asked. "The road is east, I think."

"There's someone else I need to save," Ebony said. "And you're coming with me."

"Shit," he exclaimed. "How about you drop me off somewhere safe first?"

"No dice," she said. "There's a teenager lost in the woods."

The milkman groaned.

"You can leave if you like," Ebony said. "I promise I won't stop you."

"No, I would much rather stay with you."

"That's what I thought."

21

J AYLEN FOLLOWED A BUBBLING creek for about a mile when he heard more gunshots ring off in the forest. He stopped in his tracks, trying to figure out how far they were. Perhaps it was the police or a squad of forest rangers. Either way, it made him feel hopeful, and thinking that maybe this madness would end soon.

Tobias' body was a while back, and Jaylen wasn't sure how easily he'd be able to retrace his steps. Being a black man carrying two guns in the woods in a rural part of Wisconsin didn't sound so hot, especially considering the body left behind. Luckily, there were no wounds that seemed like gunshots, but he couldn't blame it on cat creatures.

He thought it was funny that Tobias made such a fuss about these cat women, but now that Jaylen was knee-deep in the woods, he didn't see a single one. Maybe there were only a few and it wasn't that many. In that case, he had a fighting chance, especially with the Glock in his waistband and the shotgun hanging around his shoulder.

Part of him felt like he was on a suicide mission, though. His intuition served him well in the realm of making sales, particularly the zone where people were on the brink of saying yes. In those times, he felt like a shark catching the scent of blood in the water. Out here in the wilderness, he felt like a timid creature completely out of his depth and on edge. There was definitely something dangerous and he was getting closer to meeting it.

The sounds of hissing and growling assaulted his ears and the hairs on the back of his neck stood at attention. About 30 feet out, two cats that were the size of fully-grown women were fighting one another. Something about them was oddly beautiful, bordering on the edge of attractive, but within that alluring mix was a raw, primal sense of danger.

Red fur covered their curves and coiled muscles as one pounced on the other. They rolled in the dirt, and blades of grass and fallen branches flew in the air. Blood trickled down one cat woman's side, staining her fur a dark crimson.

The skinnier cat woman elbowed the cat creature beneath her, opening a fresh cut. The cat retaliated and drove her claws into the cat woman's breast, ripping it clean off. The skinnier cat howled in pain, gripping the wound as blood poured out of the opening and stained her fur a deeper shade of red.

Jaylen wasn't sure if he should back off, stay quiet or take them out before it was too late. He aimed the shotgun, watching their bodies covered in thick shadows darken. The last remaining rays of sunlight were swallowed by the woods as Jaylen pulled the trigger and hoped for the best before becoming submerged in a hazy darkness he hadn't experienced since his childhood in New Orleans.

22

B ARBARA KNEW IT WAS only a matter of time before the cat creatures would catch their scent and needed to satiate their bloodlust. The back door frame shook violently as something charged it over and over. This house stood on this land for at least a hundred years, but it was constructed with compassion and care. Raw materials that were durable and high quality, designed to stand the test of time, unlike modern-day homes that seemed to be slapped together in a few months.

This was one of many reasons Tobias and her loved living here and couldn't contemplate moving anywhere else. However, the cats seemed to be multiplying in numbers, money wasn't coming in the way it used to, and the fear of another assault was taking a toll on the couple's mental and emotional health. In their younger years, they possessed the inner strength and fortitude to withstand the trauma that came with the attacks, but now that they had reached their twilight years, they wished to spend the final leg somewhere warm and sunny near the beach.

Barbara had her heart set on Honolulu. The tropical city had good healthcare, nice beaches, and an enticing cultural scene. It would be a complete 180 from the lifestyle she was accustomed to in Wisconsin, but the change was needed. Even Tobias seemed to brighten at the prospect of leaving the farm behind them.

This dream of greener pastures muddied and darkened in her mind as she and Clara struggled to push the heavy vanity. Clara grunted and Barbara exhaled heavily as the large piece of furniture screamed across the floor, leaving large scratches in the wood floor.

The door seemed to hold much better with the weight of the vanity and no longer shook. Things almost seemed back to normal inside the farmhouse.

"We fucking did it," Clara said, putting her hand up for a high five as she tried to catch her breath.

Barbara couldn't remember the last time she high-fived someone and felt somewhat foolish doing it, but the simple gesture made her feel good.

They sat in silence on the floor, passing a bag of salty chips back and forth. The calmness and sense of security made Barbara think they might actually survive the night. The cat creatures had never dared to breach the home, so this was a first.

And then there was Clara, the only cavalry Barbara had to rely on. Something in Clara's inner world had shifted dramatically, and the girl seemed to have gained her wits. That gave Barbara a quiet sense of reassurance and made her feel like she wasn't alone in this dire predicament.

Barbara could tell Clara was wrestling with her thoughts, the girl seemed barely present and her facial expressions shifted rapidly.

"Clara, are you doing okay?" Barbara asked, worried about the poor girl.

Clara looked up, seeming surprised by the question. "W-well I–"

Her words were cut short when something violently shook the door frame once more. Barbara knew the cat women were hitting the door in a group or one of the biggest cats was charging forward. Either way, Barbara knew they had to prepare themselves for a breach.

"Pick up your knife," Barbara commanded firmly. "They're coming in any minute."

"O-okay," Clara's voice trembled as she picked up the knife and her countenance darkened.

"Give me a minute, I have a plan."

Barbara ran to the kitchen and grabbed a bag of flour.

"What is that going to do?" Clara asked as she stood, holding the blade in both hands.

"You'll see," Barbara said. "Just listen for my commands and don't lose your head."

"Can't make any promises, but I'll do my best."

"Good, that's all I want."

They both stood there, watching the vanity vibrate and the door frame crack. The vanity fell over and the glass windows shattered. A massive cat woman created a considerable hole in the back door and busted through the opening, not caring about the sharp pieces of wood cutting into her fur. Blood trickled down as she stood on her haunches and hissed.

Barbara aimed her Marlin Model 336 Classic 30-30 Winchester Satin Blued Lever Action Rifle at the cat and pulled the trigger. The hollow point ripped through the cat's chest and she fell back, yowling, clutching the wound. Blood gushed out and covered her paw as the light slowly left her eyes.

"You did it!" Clara exclaimed.

"Thanks, but we haven't made it out of hell quite yet."

Barbara signaled Clara to back up towards the stairs. They needed more room and distance. She didn't want them being ambushed or trapped and the felines moved incredibly fast.

Another one slinked through the opening, followed by another cat woman. They bent down and purred as they licked their friend's face, trying to wake her. It soon became apparent that she was dead and wouldn't be getting up. They howled and moaned in pain, tears rolling down their furry faces.

Barbara almost felt bad for them, but knew they'd rip out her throat without a moment's hesitation. Two more slipped inside the space, and she could feel Clara's questioning eyes boring into the side of her head.

Patience, dear. I have a plan.

Barbara carefully opened the flour as she heard the cries turn into growls. She tossed the bag into the center of the room, and the white powder filled the space with a smoky haze.

She aimed the gun and shot one in the head and another in the chest.

Two down, two more to go.

Tobias taught her how to shoot a range of guns in the first decade of their marriage. He told her she was a natural as she practiced shooting cans and rotten pumpkins from various distances. Firearms used to scare her, but she'd grown to like them overtime as she grew more apt and comfortable.

Barbara signaled for Clara to follow her up the stairs. Clara didn't seem to get the memo and looked paralyzed on the steps. She signaled again, knowing this wasn't the time to freeze up.

The girl still wouldn't move. Instead, she inhaled a bit of flour and sneezed, giving away their position. A cat woman pounced on Clara, and Barbara gun butted the creature with her rifle stock. It rolled down the stairs, and Barbara lifted the gun back up, aimed at the hairy creature, and fired. Blood splashed against the wall.

Barbara turned around, and felt hands shoving her down the stairs, Clara smiled devilishly as she tumbled backwards and banged her head.

23

"TAKE THIS," EBONY SAID, fishing out a pair of night vision goggles from her knapsack. She pulled out another for herself. "This is my backup pair, so don't break them."

"Thank you," the milkman said, inspecting the bulky pair of black goggles, looking at them like an alien piece of hardware.

"Hurry up and put them on," Ebony commanded, feeling somewhat nostalgic for the old days when she led small squads overseas. This was no frog, but he would have to do. Having another body on deck did give her a sense of ease, knowing her nine would be covered. "I'll press the fancy buttons for you."

"Sure thing," the milkman said, donning the apparatus on his head.

Ebony came over and clicked several buttons and knobs on the headpiece. The milkman's gear whirred to life and Ebony smiled, knowing the darkness inside his world just got that much brighter.

"This is badass," the milkman said.

"I know, right?" Ebony said. "Follow my lead and don't go rogue on me."

"You got a weapon for me?"

"Knife or gun," she asked. "What do you prefer?"

"Gun."

Ebony pulled out the Glock 20 from earlier and handed it to the milkman. He smiled in the darkness and his entire disposition seemed to relax, having a weapon in hand.

"I assume I don't need to give you a lecture or a tutorial, right?"

"Right," the milkman said. "I never served in the military, but I had plenty of family members who did and they taught me how to shoot."

"Good."

Ebony moved forward, taking point while the milkman followed. She turned back and brought her gloved finger to her lips, signaling for him to be quiet. Ever since she left the military, she'd grown accustomed to solo missions, so this felt somewhat strange to have a brother in arms, if you could call him that. The milkman seemed nice enough, but he seemed traumatized from his run-in with the cat creatures. She couldn't blame him, though; any sane person would be experiencing something similar under the same circumstances.

A gunshot rang in the distance. Ebony stopped and so did the milkman. The normal birdsong and chirping and buzzing of insects ceased and the woods were silent for a torturous moment.

Ebony had a decent ear and developed a good sense for pinpointing danger over the years. It seemed to come from up north. She signaled to move forward, and the walk transitioned into a light jog. Paying attention to her surroundings, she looked out for the cat creatures who seemed to be hidden deeper in the woods. Luckily, none of them ambushed her and the milkman.

They were getting closer, Ebony could feel it inside her gut. The dense trees cleared out, and she heard a cat hissing and a man groaning.

Moving closer, the man turned out to be the real estate agent she saw earlier in the day. He was tall, handsome, and cocky, but now he seemed frightened and out of his element. A dead cat creature lay slumped a few feet away from him. He struggled to aim his rifle; something seemed wrong with one of his shoulders.

Ebony carefully took aim, but Jaylen accidentally moved in her sights.

"Fuck," she mumbled under her breath.

Another shot whizzed past her and hit the tree behind the cat creature. The milkman took aim again, but before he could pull the trigger, the cat creature rushed him. It slashed his forehead, sleeves of blood poured down the milkman's face, and the cat creature smacked the gun out of his hand. Groaning in pain, the milkman put his hands out defensively, and the cat creature picked him up like a ragdoll, slamming him on the ground and then slamming him against a tree. Bones popped and splintered through his clothes and flesh.

Boom. Boom. Boom.

Two rounds in the head and one in the upper back did the trick, and the cat creature fell atop the milkman's dead body.

"A-are you going to kill me?" Jaylen asked.

"No, I'm not going to kill you," Ebony said.

"Well, you came to save me then?"

"No, that was happenstance or luck."

"Or God."

"If you believe in that stuff."

"I do."

"I came to save Lily."

Ebony bent down and picked up a green camera and a handful of polaroids lying next to it. It looked like it was in pretty good shape despite the grass stains covering the exterior.

She handed Jaylen the camera and looked at the physical photos. The first photo showed an innocent-looking girl with dark eyes, followed by photos of sugar maple and paper birch trees. The last photo was a close-up of a white peeling bark with several red hairs that resembled those from a cat.

"Oh my god," Jaylen exclaimed. "This is Lily's camera."

"That means she can't be too far and she might still be alive."

24

THE SOUND OF A woman screaming in pain pierced Jaylen's ears and made his heart feel like it might pop out of his chest. He hated how much creepier the night vision made the forest seem inside his optics. The green hues and white noise made him feel like he was stuck inside a shitty video game, but one without a respawn or a saved checkpoint.

Ebony moved forward, gun pointed at the sound. They rounded a tangle of trees and Jaylen almost couldn't believe his eyes. A massive male cat creature had a blonde woman bent over a log as he thrust into her soaking wet vagina. She was crying in pain, but she was smiling, white teeth gleaming in the darkness, enjoying the assault.

Was this consensual? No way is she...

She moaned in pleasure as she backed up, taking in more of his throbbing cock, veins crisscrossing the hairy shaft. He would have put a pornstar to shame and Jaylen had no idea how she was taking it so well.

The cat creature doubled down on the thrusts, aggressively growling, a paw gripping her pale ass cheek as he went deeper. The other paw/hand held her thigh and something cracked. Jaylen struggled to see what broke in the darkness.

Ebony wasted no time and let off a flurry of bullets, which landed in the beast's side. The momentary flash of light was enough for Jaylen to take in that this thing was about as big as three large bodybuilders combined. The hulking creature yelped in pain as blood trickled down its side. Those shots would have taken out one of the females, but this motherfucker was still standing. It didn't make sense.

How many more of these monsters are lurking in the woods?

The thought alone sent chills down Jaylen's spine. Ebony was a badass and a certified killer, but this monstrosity was a different breed.

The cat creature got down on all fours and charged towards Ebony. Unphased by its aggression and snarls, Ebony aimed and put two bullets directly in its forehead. It snapped back, yelping in pain as it flipped in the air and fell on its back.

"Why did you kill him?" the woman yelled, her bloodshot eyes wild, blonde hair unkempt and tangled with leaves and twigs. "That was the best lover I ever had."

As she came closer, limping, Jaylen noticed her voluptuous curves, round breasts sitting pretty, the crease of a belly button piercing, a blonde bush of hair between her toned legs. She didn't seem to care about being naked in front of others, let alone in the woods with strangers.

"That thing was dangerous," Ebony said coldly. "He was going to tear you apart at some point. Lucky, you only got your leg fucked up."

"No, you dumb cunt!" the hysterical woman yelled. "He was going to father my children."

"Listen, I don't have time for this bullshit."

"I can't believe you took him out," she said. "He was so strong, so big, so sexy."

"Well, it happened, and it's done."

"Why are you here?" the woman asked, cocking her head. "They're dangerous. No way you can take them all out."

"I have plenty of ammo and I'm here to find Lily. Have you seen a teenage girl, maybe 16-17?"

"Let's say I did, but not saying I did or didn't, what do I get out of it?"

Jaylen watched Ebony put the gun muzzle up to the blonde girl's soiled forehead. Her entire disposition shifted and she stood straight as a wooden board.

"O-okay, I'll give you whatever you want."

"The teenage girl. Bring us to her and you'll live and you can go get fucked by whatever animal you desire."

"Don't judge me!"

"Did you forget about this gun?"

"You won't kill me."

Ebony started pulling the trigger just an inch.

"Stop! I'll lead you to the girl. I'm just worked up. I didn't get to finish. My hormones are all over the place."

"Nasty," Jaylen said.

Ebony pulled the gun away from the girl's head and her shoulders relaxed. She took a step forward and collapsed, howling in pain.

"My fucking leg. I don't think I can walk."

"Can you point us in the right direction?" Ebony asked, her face visibly unconcerned with the girl's pain.

Jaylen felt bad for the girl, but he didn't have an emergency medical pack on hand or the medical knowledge on how to fix a broken leg. Even with night vision, the damage seemed pretty bad. He was surprised she was able to stand at all, considering what she had just gone through.

He thought about how much she was enjoying getting fucked by that monstrosity and almost threw up. *What would make a person want to go through those types of lengths to get laid? Whatever happened to just having sex with a man or a human? Must be cuckoo to even stay in these woods and let that thing touch you.*

The blonde pointed past the monstrosity's dead body into the darkness. "She's by the stream. Can't tell if she's sleeping or unconscious. Really not my problem."

"Are you lying?" Ebony asked. "If you are, I'll come back and test out my new knife on you."

The blonde shook her head intensely. "N-no, I promise I'm telling the truth. Swear to God."

"Alright," Ebony said. "Taking your word for it."

Jaylen followed Ebony as they walked deeper into the forest, which somehow seemed even creepier at night.

I'm not supposed to be here. I'm just a real estate agent. Nala will barely believe it. Might think I made the whole thing up, that is, if I survive the night.

Despite the cold air, Jaylen could feel the sweat in the small of his back and his underarms. He would have changed out of this suit a long time ago, considering how torn up and worn it had become in such a short time. A hot shower and the heat of Nala's body would melt all his troubles away, but these seemed like fantastical images, a pipedream. Surviving this ordeal might as well be a long shot.

Sure, Ebony was unstoppable, but Jaylen was just a man who barely knew how to shoot. Yes, he told the truth when he mentioned his folks teaching him the basics, but that was decades ago. It wasn't rocket science, but he needed to be a sure shot, not just a decent marksman.

The stream of water bubbled and whooshed past Jaylen. He wondered if it was clean enough to drink or if contaminants had found this water and corrupted its pure essence into something other.

Ebony and he combed the surrounding area for any bodies, but nothing seemed to be off. That was until he noticed something off in a pile of leaves.

"Lily," Jaylen said in a soft voice, not wanting to startle the pale girl. "Wake up. We're here to help you and bring you back to safety."

The girl was nonresponsive. Ebony watched patiently in the background, keeping her head on a swivel in case any of the cat creatures wanted to run up on them. Jaylen lightly shook her shoulder and gently touched her face. She was cold and her cheeks seemed so pale. He wasn't sure how long she'd been lying here; but he didn't want her to catch anything.

"Might have to pick her up," Ebony suggested.

"Maybe we should call an ambulance," Jaylen said.

"Not a bad idea, but not until we get her out of these damn woods. We don't want to be sitting ducks."

"Got you."

Ebony came over and helped him pick the girl up. He wrapped her in his blazer and laid her over his good shoulder. They started trekking back, tracing the path that led them here when the blonde shrieked and attacked Ebony with a sharp stick.

She grabbed the girl's wrist, twisted it, and Jaylen heard a sickening crack.

"What did I tell you?" Ebony said, her voice sharp. "I'm not a joke."

"Fuck you," the blonde said, spitting in Ebony's face.

Ebony jabbed her in the chest and followed it up by a right cross to the jaw, which put the blonde on her ass. Blood gushed out the wound and she started crying hysterically.

"I-I just want to get fucked."

"You stay out here, and you'll get fucked in every sense of the word," Ebony said.

The blonde didn't even register Ebony's words, wallowing in her own world of self-pity and desperation.

"Suit yourself."

Jaylen and Ebony left the blonde behind, still hearing her howls and cries ring through the forest like a bird's death cry.

25

C LARA WATCHED THE OLD lady tumble down the stairs as she gripped the railing. With her other hand, she held tightly onto the butcher knife. Her heart ached, but another, darker part of her gained a grim sense of satisfaction from the action. She had intrusive thoughts from time to time that were violent and strange, which she suppressed, but indulging in this one felt amazing.

Titillated by the momentary sense of power, she came back to her senses and realized she was still vulnerable. The cat creature had gained access to the back of the farmhouse and here she was standing on the staircase looking like prey. She ran up the stairs, unsure of where she was going. Having no real plan, she told herself that she would figure it out.

Hide, Clara, hide. Shrink into a small ball. You've done that your entire marriage. Hide in plain sight. This isn't any different.

Her stomach clenched, thinking about all the times she silenced herself and shrank in the presence of her husband. She had liked the idea of being a traditional housewife and falling into preconceived gender roles. But she still had dreams and ambitions that she folded and filed away in the darkest recesses of herself that she could find.

A tear ran down her cheek as she continued up the stairs, struggling to process her emotions and make sense of the layout of the house. A string hung down from the ceiling, which meant there was an attic. On the other hand, there were a couple of cracked doors, which lined the hallway. She assumed one was the master bedroom and the other was a guest bedroom or possibly even a bathroom.

Which one? Which one? Do I go to the attic and hide or barricade myself in the bedroom?

Clara heard purring downstairs. Her heart thumped in her chest harder than a boxer's jab. She had to hurry up and make a decision, but her mind raced. This was a time where Oliver would decide for her, but the bastard was dead. She had the power of choice and time was dwindling.

Attic.

She yanked on the white string and a set of stairs came down. Darkness obscured the entrance and she gulped before climbing up. She couldn't remember the last time she'd been inside an attic and second guessed her decision. It was too late to turn back now. Cobwebs stretched across her face and broke as she waded into the dark space and her vision struggled to adjust to it. She pulled the stairs up until the light beneath her was swallowed up.

Wrapping her arms around her legs, she buried her face into her knees and rocked back and forth, the knife trembling in her hand while holding onto the hope that those wretched things wouldn't find her.

26

D ARK SHAPES SCURRIED IN the dense canopy above Ebony, Jaylen, and Lily. The tree branches creaked and groaned with the weight of the cat creatures. Even with the advanced night vision, she struggled to see what was going on in the darkness.

They had the high ground advantage, fighting from an elevated position: a wider field of vision, the defensive upper hand, range and force, and melee benefits.

She felt fucked. If she had a squad of Navy Seals with her, she'd breathe a lot easier, but Jaylen was a real estate agent and Lily was an unconscious teenage girl. Things were looking dire, but Ebony wasn't one to just give up or give in when things got rough.

She aimed her gun upward, pointing into the darkness, knowing she'd be able to mow some of these bitches down, but she had no idea how many she was dealing with. Based on the constant movement, it sounded like *lots*, maybe an entire militia of cryptids. She had read somewhere that a group of feral cats was sometimes called a destruction. And the term seemed accurate because that's exactly what she felt was coming.

A few jumped down from the trees, hidden inside the thick terrain. She struggled to make out how many were creeping towards her and her team.

More dark shapes jumped down, barely making a sound in the leaves. They didn't purr or make any verbal noises. Ebony's throat was dry and her tongue felt like a weight inside her mouth. Part of her was itching for some action, waiting for them to make the first move. Her patience was wearing thin and her adrenaline was about to start flowing.

Several of them rushed her, coming into view. Rounds penetrated the crowd and she pulled a grenade out of her pocket, biting the pin off, spitting it out, and throwing it deeper into the woods.

Before it went off, she yelled back at Jaylen. "Get the fuck out of here and bring Lily back to the farmhouse. I got it from here."

"But what about—"

"That was not a question, that was a muthafuckin command."

"Roger that."

Jaylen started moving away from Ebony with Lily slumped over his shoulder like a bag of mulch. She exhaled, but tensed when the grenade went off and a vivid flash of white exploded in her vision, lighting up the lush environment.

Skull fragments whizzed past Ebony's head like shrapnel, a hind leg careened into the treetops, several ribcages, spines, tails, paws, and viscera flew into the air like confetti.

A cat creature with singed fur that somehow survived the explosion, bit into Ebony's forearm. The burnt fur smelled pungent, sharp, and acrid. Ebony nearly dropped her gun, and she kicked the cat's thin ankle. It instantly released its canines and Ebony grabbed the back of its head, part of her hand gripping fur that fell like blackened ash to the earth while two fingers clutched a pointed ear, and slammed its face into a tree, muzzle crushed like a soda can. Blood squirted out the wound as she yowled.

Ebony wondered if the stinging bite on her arm would leave a scar or infect her in the next couple of days. The thought alone pissed her off so much she slammed the cat's face into the bark over and over until it went limp.

Another cat jumped on her from behind and she struggled to get it off. Sharp claws dug into the musculature of her back, tearing through multiple layers of clothing and protective gear. Ebony ran backwards into a thick tree, hearing the cat creature yelp in pain. Ebony threw a mean uppercut at the big cat before it could get up, preferring to use her hands rather than her gun, strapped around her body.

She grabbed the cat's furry head, placing one hand over an ear and the other beneath its chin, getting a good grip. The dazed cat began coming back to its senses and Ebony snapped its neck. The sound was sickening, but the *crack* made her feel alive, in tune with the natural ebb and flow of nature's vicious rhythms.

Things seemed to quiet down a moment, but her adrenaline was still flowing. She hoped she didn't take them all out so swiftly. She needed a full body intact, parts and all for Tatou. And she wasn't going to drag the male creature's massive body either. This question was answered when she saw more shapes pounce down from the trees, lean fast twitch muscles allowing them to land on their feet so softly.

Ebony kissed her M4A1 carbine, knowing that she had started a war that she planned to end before the sun rose.

27

J AYLEN WAS THANKFUL HE started lifting weights a few times a week inside his garage. He had a bench press, some dumbbells, and two kettlebells. He'd become enamored with his black iron Versace kettlebells imprinted with the Medusa face.

Kettlebell swings had become his favorite workout and made him feel like he was doing something worthwhile. At first, it was strange and annoying, attempting to get the swings right. His arms feeling off balance and gravity doing its job, however; he quickly improved, and the vigorous workout became meditative.

His upper body became leaner and more muscular, and his strength improved. It was a great break from showing homes, selling property, and looking over piles of paperwork.

The girl didn't weigh much, but he knew he and Ebony covered a great distance over time. It felt strange not checking his black Santos De Cartier watch with the black alligator leather strap wrapped around his wrist. The night vision was good, but it wasn't good enough to tell him where the steel-shaped hands pointed on his watch face. And even if he didn't have night vision, there was no way he'd be able to see the time in the darkness.

These thoughts sounded stupid and vain, but he couldn't help it. Outside of family, all he cared about was money and materialistic things. Part of him felt ashamed for putting so much energy into this avenue, but his ego lived for it. That 200k commission wasn't off the table either. Something deep inside him felt like he could make it happen, even with the odds stacked against him. Having Lily in tow made him feel like he could make it through the night and make this sale a reality. Reuniting the girl with her parents had to count for something. They might buy the property out of goodwill and thankfulness.

He knew this was wishful thinking to some degree, but it helped him as he continued moving forward, hearing gunshots rattling off in the distance. That explosion was almost deafening; his ears took a moment to readjust. He'd never heard any sort of bomb go off in his life, only on tv or in video games.

Growing tired, he wished he could go to sleep, but he had to keep moving. Didn't want to run into one of those cat creatures caught off guard and had to get this girl to safety. There was no other way, the girl was his responsibility.

Pain shot through his other shoulder, and he wondered how bad it was. Earlier, he'd killed one of the cat creatures off a lucky shot and the other one lunged at him. The bitch was strong and ferocious, pinning him to the ground, her weight leaning on his shoulder and he heard a *pop*.

He thanked God that Ebony showed up and killed her. Otherwise, he'd surely be dead and not walking through these woods like a zombie on a mission.

More gunshots went off in the darkness, jolting Jaylen and waking him up on deeper levels. He adjusted his grip on Lily's legs, grunted, and tightened his other hand around his gun. He wondered about his wife Nala and his two daughters, imagining them going through their daily routines and wondered if they felt his absence. His stomach hurt, yearning to feel his daughters' hugs, and his wife's warm skin as they cuddled together at night, wrapped up in each other like a pretzel. He wondered how much longer he had to endure this horrific night and how much longer he'd have to wait to be reunited with his family.

28

B ARBARA COUGHED, STRUGGLING TO come to, feeling out of place for a second before remembering what had led to her falling down the stairs.

That bitch, Clara.

She consoled the woman, listened to her vent for what seemed like hours, gave her a literal shoulder to cry on and she pushed her down the stairs.

What happened to respect for the elderly? She wouldn't dare treat someone like that at Clara's age. That's part of the reason she enjoyed living in isolation and being on a farm. Something dark and malignant had taken hold of society and was gnawing away at everything good. She wanted no part of it.

Barbara's body ached all over and hip throbbed with a sharp pain. She didn't know where the cat women could have gone and her vision was a bit blurry. Blinking over and over, her vision slowly came back into focus and she saw a thin layer of flour coating the floor and the bodies she had taken out.

Where are the cats and how am I alive?

As if they could read her thoughts, Barbara heard chaotic movement upstairs, several claws scratching wood, and a groaning. It sounded like they were in the attic and she wondered if the ungrateful girl had gone up there to hide. Not a terrible idea, but she didn't have much sense and probably deserved whatever terrible fate was coming her way.

Barbara didn't have time to worry about the commotion. She had to move somewhere safe and secure or at the very least find a weapon. She searched the ground for her gun, but it was nowhere in sight. Her neck and upper back itched something fierce. This happened to her on occasion whenever she was anxious and nervous, but it was exacerbated by the flour that had coated her skin like thick makeup.

She walked into the kitchen as quickly as she could. Grabbing a knife, and feeling the weight of it felt silly. There was no way she was going to be able to take out all of them by herself with a mere knife. Surveying the kitchen, her eyes kept returning to the kitchen sink.

Water. Cats hate water.

Barbara grabbed the faucet hose and readied herself. Two cat creatures came bounding down the stairs, loud as hell, growling on the entire descent. Her hands shook as she clutched it with both hands. Their orange eyes glared with rage and hate as they lunged. She pulled the trigger and sprayed the felines, who growled as the water soaked their fur.

Momentarily blinded and rolling on the floor, Barbara took a dutch oven off the counter, struggling to balance the weight with her shaky arm. She dropped it on the cat woman's head, and it yowled in pain, blood leaking from its smashed eye and broken nasal bones. Wasting no time, Barbara picked it up and let it drop down with force behind it. The cat woman's face caved in.

Barbara wanted to celebrate, wishing Tobias was here to appreciate her successful kill. He would have been worried and proud at the same time. She didn't have too much time to indulge this fantasy because the other cat woman was getting up, shaking the water from her red fur.

Thinking on her feet, Barbara pulled open a drawer, digging through kitchen utensils and settled on a marble rolling pin. This was a gift from another farmer's wife named Grace. They'd hang out on occasion, sharing town gossip and pleasantries. She was thankful for the kitchen tool and readied herself. The cat woman was quicker than Barbara thought, running directly for her, pivoting at the last moment and leaping off the wall.

Closing her eyes, Barbara swung, hoping for the best, feeling completely off kilter. The rolling pin connected with the cat woman's underbelly, cracking a few ribs. It collapsed, gripping its stomach, purring in pain.

Feeling confident, Barbara walked over, ready to finish the job. The cat woman struck Barbara's ankle and she fell, dropping the kitchen tool, helplessly watching it roll away from her. She screamed until her throat hurt, watching the cat lean over her.

The cat woman's eyes seemed to glow like fiery orbs as she bared her sharp yellowed teeth. Fear clutched Barbara and her heart drummed inside her chest. She jabbed the cat's muzzle before gripping a handful of whiskers in each fist and pulling with every ounce of her strength. The cat woman yelped in pain as Barbara ripped them out and tossed them aside. Small rivers of red opened up on the cat woman's face, hair follicles bleeding profusely.

Pawing her own face, the cat woman struggled to staunch the bleeding and yowled. The cries of distress and pain hurt Barbara's ears, but jolted her into action. She rolled off her back, watching the cat woman move in a disoriented fashion, bumping into the wall and then bumping into a stool.

Barbara scrambled to pick up the rolling pin, knowing she didn't have too much time. She scooped it up, noticing a pool of blood forming on the floor, dripping down the cat woman's muzzle. She swung and nearly missed the cat woman's head. Her body ached from the exertion and she wished she could rest.

Instead, she readjusted her form and swung as hard as she could, hitting its spine. The cat woman yelped so loudly, Barbara almost dropped the object. She struck its back again, hearing something break. Before she could strike it again, another cat woman swiped her forearm, ripping through fabric and flesh. The rolling pin clattered to the ground and Barbara instinctively gripped the wound.

Four more cat women walked upright behind the one who scratched her. Tears formed at the corners of Barbara's eyes and she wished she could hug Tobias one more time. She knew they'd kissed passionately before going their separate ways, but she was confident that her husband would return in one piece. Grief washed over her in waves, feeling the full reality of knowing that he was gone and that she wouldn't be seeing tomorrow either.

The cat woman slashed at Barbara's shoulder and stomach, opening large gashes, blood seeping out in sheets. She fell to her knees, coughing up blood. Feeling an intense heat ransack her body, she hallucinated a beach, a beautiful shore and soft waves tickling her feet. The cat women closed in on her and the heat expanded, she swore she could feel Tobias' hand grip her own and his soft lips kiss her forehead, and his beard hair scratch her chin as more claws rained down and the heat swallowed her into a warm oblivion.

29

E BONY THOUGHT SHE KILLED an entire platoon's worth of cat cryptids, but the fuckers kept coming in droves. At this rate, she was going to run out of ammo.

She didn't mind using knives, but in this situation, guns were preferable. Droves of cats streamed out of the trees and memories of being stationed in Rota, Spain drifted into her mind. It was one of the few times she didn't have to worry about war. It was a chill base, but they had a cat problem. You'd hear cats lounging around the dumpsters, purring loudly as they mated. They reproduced exponentially and the base was flooded with feral cats. The local town brought in a team who exterminated a large portion of the cats and things returned to normal.

Ebony wondered if the exterminator felt the same way she did at this moment. It was a grim job, the hard labor of putting these cats down. She was sure putting down innocent cats on a Naval base had to be ten times harder, considering they had no way to defend themselves and she figured the people had empathy for the creatures.

Ebony, on the other hand, didn't feel a shred of empathy for the cat women. They were dangerous and determined to take her out.

Her shoulder ached as she continued pouring round after round into the swarms of big cats, tearing them apart. A couple of them dodged the bullet spray, shielded by the bodies of their fallen sisters.

One swept her legs while the other one swatted the assault rifle out of her hands. Ebony elbowed one in the face and pulled out the Smith & Wesson HRT fixed blade boot knife from the nylon sheath adorning her ankle. The small blade didn't seem like much, but Ebony sliced the cat creature's stomach in a wide arc, watching its steaming entrails slide out. The other one bared its teeth before charging her and she side-stepped its attack, slicing its ankle. It fell to the side, skidding into the dirt.

Ebony stomped down on the injured ankle and kicked the cat in the stomach. It yelled in pain. She jabbed the knife into the cat's throat. Before she could catch a break, another was on her back, digging its claws into her chest.

Slicing the right paw, blood gushed out and the cat creature released its hold. Ebony turned around and hit the creature with a roundhouse kick. More flashes of fur sped through her peripheral, and she took a deep breath. One leapt in the air and she drove the blade under its jaw, gutting its snout and savagely dislodging the weapon. She plunged it in the creature's eye and it got stuck in the oral cavity, most likely lodged between the muscle tissue and bone.

No point in holding onto what is lost.

Ebony dug into her shirt, closing her fingers around the Karambit Flipper Black Hawkbill Blade inside her bra. Her fingers snugly moved into the grooves and she held the blade similar to brass knuckles. She dove into a forward roll, coming to her knees and slicing in a circular motion, the stainless steel cutting through thighs and legs. Blood sprayed Ebony's face, speckling her stoic countenance in a crimson red.

She didn't look away. She focused on the task and continued cutting the cat creatures down. One bit into her shoulder and another punched her in the stomach. The wind rushed out of Ebony's lungs, the blade fell from her hands and she grew dizzy. Breathing in through her nostrils, she went with the flow of things, remaining neutral instead of sliding into panic mode.

Embracing the pain, Ebony allowed it to serve as an anchor, grounding herself in her body, and bringing her deeper into the moment. The sharp teeth sank deeper into her shoulder meat and she grabbed the cat creature's head as she bent down in fluid motion, bringing it over her shoulder and slamming it down in a clean half circle.

Ebony wasted no time stomping its throat in and spinning into a backfist that connected with a cat creature's face, breaking its wet pink nose. She fished out a long blade from her forearm, one that Chef Hirayama kindly asked her to test out.

A cat creature's tail swayed from side to side and it stood there grinning, waiting for Ebony to make the first move. It purred seductively, rubbing its own breasts. Something about its movements made Ebony feel sleepy in a sense, more relaxed. It moved closer, running its claws down its own stomach.

Ebony's breath hitched in her own throat and felt strangely attracted to the beast. She never liked the opposite sex and never experimented with women, but the beast was oozing with sexual charm. She remembered the blonde getting fucked by the massive male cat creature and her pussy grew wet with excitement. Part of her wanted to rip her own clothes off, but she was going with the flow, allowing things to play out.

The cat creature came closer, caressing Ebony's cheek. Her body flushed with excitement. A plane roared overhead and the cat creature looked up at the sky. Ebony returned to her senses, thankful for the fortunate distraction and embraced the repulsion she felt for the cryptids. She slid forward and went for a calf kick. The cat creature dodged the blow and punched her in the gut and followed it up with a jab cross combo to the face. A small cut opened in Ebony's cheek and she tasted blood.

She spat into the grass and jabbed the blade into the cat's chest plate, quickly took it out and sliced the connective tissue and ligaments holding its elbow and forearm together. Blood spilled and it cried out in pain, holding the limb dangling from a thread of sinew and tendons.

Ebony sliced its back in a X motion, until the cat creature collapsed. Two other cat creatures fled into the woods, retreating.

Compliments to the chef.

Chef Hirayama would be pleased to know how well his blade worked and how much it assisted her in the heat of combat. It was lightweight, durable, and most of all, deadly.

Ebony couldn't believe the number of bodies and parts covering the forest floor. She waited for more to come crawling down from the trees, but after some time passed, nothing did.

She picked up her gun off the ground, but deep claw marks were embedded in the stock and barrel. The optic sight was smashed into pieces and all that remained was the attachment mount. The trigger was warped and parts of the gun looked as if they had been physically bent the wrong way slightly.

The gun was useless to her now.

She dropped it, remembering that she still had her HK 45 semi-automatic pistol holstered if she needed it.

Ebony grabbed a cryptid that was dead, but not in terrible shape, by the legs. She began dragging it behind her as she began her trek back to the farm. She sighed, hoping Lily and Jaylen were okay.

30

E BONY LIMPED AND JAYLEN gritted his teeth, carrying the weight of Lily's body on his shoulder. She was small, but that weight seemed to have ballooned with every step taken.

They moved in silence towards the farmhouse, but something seemed to have shifted when they approached the quaint building. The atmosphere felt off, as if the calm nature of the property was stripped away and replaced by a feral undercurrent.

Something squished under Jaylen's foot, and he looked at the black sole of his Ferragamos and saw the remains of what seemed to be an eyeball.

"What type of sick shit is this?" Jaylen asked.

He scraped his shoes on the grass, making sure to wipe the ocular sphere off completely. This seemed like an omen, something the older black women in Baton Rouge would whisper about at night while his dad played cards with the other men, gambling away hard-earned money.

Ebony took point once again while Jaylen followed. He wasn't sure how the woman was still alive, streaks of blood painting her face like warpaint, but she was a killing machine and he was thankful they were on the same side. He couldn't imagine crossing someone like her; it would be a certified death wish.

The front door was unlocked, swinging open as Ebony pushed it open with the tip of her pistol and flashlight. Nothing strange in the foyer. Everything seemed where it was supposed to be, but Jaylen kept looking behind him, expecting a pack of the cat creatures to come running after them. They moved into the kitchen.

"Barbara," Ebony called.

Two dead cat creatures were slumped over one another and Barbara's bloody body was hunched over the sink, flaps of skin hanging off her neck and face exposing musculature. Her damaged face almost seemed like a mask ready to slide off.

"Poor woman," Ebony said.

Jaylen solemnly nodded.

"Be on the lookout," Ebony warned. "Could be a couple more of 'em lurking in the house."

"Sure thing."

Ebony took the lead and Jaylen followed her as they moved into the back of the house. Multiple cat creatures were dead and lying on the floor. There was a light coating of something beige blanketing everything.

"Looks like flour," Ebony said, almost reading Jaylen's mind.

"I don't understand."

"Crazy things happen in firefights and war."

Jaylen nodded, still struggling to wrap his head around how flour came into the equation. It made no sense to him. Was Barbara baking something when they were attacked? Nothing was laid out in the kitchen and the oven was off.

How strange...

A huge hole decorated the back door, tufts of red fur hung off the sharp edges and splotches of blood dotted the surface.

"Upstairs," Ebony said. "We have to clear the house."

"Okay," Jaylen said. He didn't think they *had* to do anything, but he wasn't going to argue with Ebony. He knew it was almost over.

They moved up the stairs and something groaned above them. He wasn't sure if it was the old house settling or a cat creature waiting in the wings, but he figured it was probably one of the cryptids. He wanted to set Lily down, but didn't want her to be attacked while they were upstairs, exploring the rooms.

Ebony moved through the rooms like a soldier, clearing out a house. Jaylen had seen shaky videos online of squads doing the same thing and he'd wondered what types of fucked up shit she had seen and been through during her service.

The rooms were curiously empty and Jaylen felt as if maybe they could relax. Something thumped above them and a set of stairs swung down. Clara's dead body came tumbling down, right arm snapping on impact. She was nude and scratched beyond belief, deep gouges in her body like red tattoos.

"F–"

"Shush," Ebony hissed.

Jaylen nodded and aimed his gun, ready for anything to happen.

Ebony pointed her gun into the darkness and another body dropped down, this one a dead cat creature, throwing her off balance. She grunted as she tossed it off her chest, coughing out hair. A blue heel was stuck inside the cat creature's ocular cavity, dried blood spiderwebbing outward.

Jaylen thought maybe he could let his guard down and took a breath as red fur flashed in his vision as a cat creature lunged out of the darkness. It coiled its back, hissing. Jaylen pulled the trigger, but missed, rounds puncturing the wall behind it.

Ebony took aim, but the cat creature leapt across the wall, claws leaving deep scratches in the wood, and jumped on top of the weapon. The gun fell from her hands and skidded across the floor.

The big cat swiped at Ebony and she leaned back, narrowly avoiding the blow. She jabbed the cat, took its head and slammed it onto her knee. It moaned in agony, blood spilling down its snout, reeling backwards.

Ebony pulled out a knife from her sleeve, brandishing it like an old friend. Jaylen watched in awe and fear at the display.

The big cat creature charged again, knocking Ebony off her feet. It slashed her stomach and Ebony sliced its thigh. It rolled to the side, holding the wound. Ebony kicked it in the face, pinned it down with her knees, raised the knife above her head and plunged it into the thing's chest over and over. Blood squirted from the chest cavity and life left the cat creature's fierce eyes.

Breathing heavily, Ebony stood and recovered both her pistol and flashlight from the ground. She walked up the stairs into the attic and explored the space.

She yelled. "Clear!"

Ebony came back down, and Jaylen felt like he could breathe again. They went back down the stairs and exited through the front door.

"It's over, thank God, it's over," Jaylen said.

Something roared in the forest and Jaylen groaned. "What the fuck is that? I thought you killed them all."

Ebony laughed. "I killed a good chunk of them, greatly reducing their numbers, but I know there's more."

Jaylen shivered at the thought. "You think there's more of those big motherfuckers? The cat men?"

"Afraid so, but we don't need to stay here and be the welcoming committee. Far as I'm concerned, my job is done and so is yours."

"But what about the people in town?"

"Listen, I'm out of ammo, I'm exhausted and I'm a hunter, not a hero. They'll have to figure this shit out."

"Yeah, that's logical, but I still have business that needs to be taken care of before I dip out."

Jaylen still didn't lose sight of the money that was floating in the air. His prospective buyers and the owners were dead, but that didn't mean he couldn't salvage this sale.

Ebony shrugged and headed back outside towards her truck. Jaylen followed with Lily still draped over his shoulder. He gently set the body of the teenage girl in the passenger seat, thankful to be unburdened by the weight and responsibility. Ebony moved to the back of her truck and wrapped the dead cryptid she dragged from the woods in a beige tarp and placed two thick slabs of concrete on top of it.

"Are those necessary?" Jaylen asked.

"In my line of work, yeah. You wouldn't believe the stories I have and the things I've seen."

"After this week, I might believe anything."

31

T ATOU'S EYES LIT UP when Ebony unveiled the dead cryptid, limp and lifeless in the same soiled tarp that she wrapped it in last week. Blood stained the tarp, but the feline cryptid was still in incredible shape. It was about 5 ft 7 inches, a pink nose, long whiskers, large breasts, coiled muscle, hips, and toned legs covered in several layers of red fur. Decay seemed to set in much more slowly compared to humans.

"This specimen is so much more beautiful than I could have imagined," Tatou said, moving close and inhaling the scent from the dead cryptid like a freshly lit candle.

"Glad you're happy with the results."

"I'm quite pleased," she said, pulling a twig out of the cryptid's fur and tossing it aside. "You know we have a saying in French, *Avoir une araignée au plafond,* and it fits you well."

"What does it mean?" Ebony asked, her curiosity piqued.

"To have a spider on a ceiling."

"There aren't any spiders in here," Ebony said, scanning the ceiling above her. The place seemed spotless and assumed the woman had an entire cleaning staff.

"No, it's a colloquialism, and I promise you there are many spiders in here," Tatou said, pointing an index finger at her own head. "I say that to say you're batshit crazy, but I appreciate it."

Ebony laughed, taking no offense whatsoever to the statement. "This isn't the first time someone has called me crazy. And I admit it, I have spiders on my ceiling, but I embrace it."

"As you should," Tatou said, caressing the cat creature's face, the side of her hand brushing the whiskers like a comb. "I have a proposition for you…"

Ebony noticed a gleam in the French woman's eye that made her stomach churn. "Go on…"

"How do you feel about going back and getting a male specimen?" Tatou grabbed the cryptid's dark paw and lightly massaged its palm.

Ebony's body hurt all over again, a painful reminder of what she had to endure to acquire this cryptid for her employer. Part of her had mentally walked out of the luxurious apartment, slipped back inside her rental car, revved the engine, and sped off. Yet the rest of her was still here, willing to hear Tatou's proposition. Money and another adrenaline rush was on the table, and Ebony didn't want to miss out on a potentially good opportunity.

"So soon though?"

"I'll triple your pay, and give you whatever weaponry is needed," Tatou said.

"What's the catch?" Ebony asked, her gut clenched, an intuitive signal that whatever Tatou would say next was going to make her kiss her teeth.

"Ebony, forever perceptive," Tatou trailed her index finger down the cat creature's forehead, sliding it over the nose, over its mouth and chin, speeding across the throat and clavicle, until it came to a sudden stop on its heart. "You have to bring it back alive."

Ebony sighed and her stomach dropped, but the money and the challenge of bringing back a cryptid alive sparked a small flame of excitement in her gut that grew exponentially. She'd bought back a live chupacabra to another employer years ago, but most people were fine with simply owning one even if it was dead. The wealthy liked to show off these creatures as trophies, symbols of immense power and excess.

Tatou had a different outlook and deep pockets, two things Ebony respected. Perhaps this could be a new peak she could overcome, she just needed to do the proper preparation and legwork.

"So, what do you say? Are you ready for another hunt?"

"I almost can't believe I'm saying this, but I'm down."

"Wonderful," Tatou beamed, pulling Ebony into a warm hug. The French woman smelled yeasty, tangy with hints of tarragon. "I knew you would be up to the challenge."

32

J AYLEN COULDN'T BELIEVE HE made it through the night. He passed out in his car, but not before concocting partial schemes and loose plans as to how he could still make the sale work. The legalities made his stomach hurt, but he wasn't a loser. He was going to make this work even if he had to get his hands dirty.

There were already several missed calls from his wife Nala and he couldn't help but groan at seeing them, knowing he was going to get an earful from her when he finally called back. Still, he had to make this count; he couldn't come home with nothing to show for it. Making a couple of quick phone calls, he extended his stay at the hotel and changed his return flight home.

A week that's all I need.

Jaylen got out of the car and walked inside the Hollis home with his hand wrapped around his Glock. He wasn't sure if doing this was stupid, brave or ambitious, but he was determined to make the sale happen.

The place reeked of animals and death. After doing a thorough walk-through, he realized he was safe, at least for the moment. He pulled the paperwork out of a manila folder, inspecting the files that had already been signed by the old couple. Part of him felt bad for them and how they went out, but another part of him reasoned that they didn't have much longer left, considering their age.

Everyone has an expiration date. I got plenty of time left on my clock.

Jaylen looked at the unsigned documents and had a bright idea. He found Barbara's body and shoved a pen inside her palm, closing his hand around the cold fingers. Guiding her hand was relatively easy, but his stomach churned throughout the process as he forged her signature.

"Just like that, Mrs. Hollis. Thank you for your signature."

Smiling, he shuffled the papers and put them away before going into the bathroom and scrubbing his hands with soap and water. He looked at the sun shining through the window and felt like things might actually work out.

Now what to do about these bodies?

ACKNOWLEDGEMENTS

I want to give special thanks to Tierra T. Ellis for the constant support, encouragement, inspiration, helping me get rid of bad ideas, and listening to me talk about this book from every angle. I want to thank the Broken River Collective: E. Rathke, David Simmons, Kelby Losack, and J. David Osborne for pushing me outside my comfort zone, craft talk, and encouragement. And thanks to Xavier Garcia for editing this book and helping bring the high strangeness to the forefront.

Grant Wamack is a Navy veteran and the author of *The Frolicking, Bullet Tooth,* and *God's Leftovers,* among other novels. He has more than forty short stories published in places such as *Dark Moon Digest, Bruiser Mag,* and *The New Flesh.* When he's not writing, he's reading tarot cards, practicing jiu jitsu, and floating around LA. You can follow his come-up over at his newsletter Literary Loud: https://grantwamack.substack.com/

www.ingramcontent.com/pod-product-compliance
Lightning Source LLC
Chambersburg PA
CBHW051255250626
47155CB00009B/3295